LOVE Ya BABY

Gary Sanders

DEDICATION

This book is dedicated to the man known in my family as Papa. Elmer Greer (our Papa) was my maternal grandfather & although he left us much too soon he did so only after imparting important life lessons.

He taught me at an early age that there is nothing more useful than a powerful story, well told. I have used that skill many times to extract myself from bad situations & I base my writing on it as well

ACKNOWLEDGMENTS

over design by ~ idrewdesign & David Black

Editing by indieauthorcounsel.com

My son, Jason Sanders is the motivation for & the only reason there is a book here to read. He convinced me that the time was right for the world outside of Hollywood to read my work. Jason has been my researcher, advisor & voice of reason on this project. I am truly blessed to have not only a son I am very proud of, but also a son who is my best friend.

This book would not have been possible without the tireless efforts of my good friend David Black & his production company Maldenite Productions at maldenite.com. His contributions have included layout & design, formatting, typing, technical & moral support, as well as camera work & editing for our video book trailers. He has been a consummate pro & a true brother in arms in every regard.

Elena

The sounds of the man's screams coming through Sonny's open window were soul-scorching. Sonny Calderone pushed the black Escalade around the corner and further into the night. He had to find Elena and, just maybe, he would have a shot at ending the screaming man's suffering. He was pretty sure the cries of pain coming from inside the burning barrel were from Rico, one of his informants. The message of the screams was meant for him and came special delivery, compliments of Cisco Ruiz, or *El Gato* (the cat), as the locals called him. Forget about Elena. Back off or die! This was Cisco's message.

Sonny could remember the days when a drug kingpin wouldn't dare risk killing a DEA agent. Those days were ancient history now. It didn't matter though. Forgetting Elena was not something Sonny Calderone could ever do, for two reasons. Number one, and the reason that mattered most to Sonny right now, was the fact that he loved Elena more than life itself. Sonny took a powerful swig from a half-empty tequila bottle and ran his finger across the snapshot of Elena he kept stuck to his dash. Besides love, he was duty bound. She was his informant, his C.I. One he had risked considerable assets to put into place.

As he turned the next corner, his headlights picked up two men rolling a burning barrel into the middle of the road. They squirted lighter fluid into the barrel causing the flames and the screams to leap higher, and then quickly disappeared into the darkness. Sonny put the Escalade into a slide that stopped next to the barrel, and rushed out from behind the wheel. The screams had less force now but they were just as shrill. Sonny did a quick scan to check for anyone that might have him in their sights. Then, stiff armed, he pointed his nine millimeter into the flaming barrel at Rico's sizzling head. He squeezed off three quick rounds and the shrieking stopped.

El Guiso, or 'the burn,' was something any school girl in this border town of Reynosa, Mexico, could tell you about. It was commonly used by the Zetas and the Gulf cartel on their enemies. They dumped a person into a big steel barrel, doused him with gasoline, and then tossed in a match. The screams were a reminder to all *paisanos.* "Cross the cartel and you would join this poor martyr in a living, dying, burning hell much more real than the one the church threatened."

Sonny had joined the DEA fifteen years earlier, straight out of the Marines for all the right reasons. Love of country...duty...honor those kinds of things. It was his Hispanic heritage and his bi-lingual abilities as much as anything that got him the job. The focus then, as now, was on south Texas where fifty percent of all illicit drugs enter the United States.

"Bust quantity and you'll move up fast," his boss had told him.

"The future of this agency is ours." That was the inside word among Latinos in the department then. Sonny closed his eyes and pictured Elena's smile and easy laughter. He was a fool to let her stay undercover after Cisco Ruiz fell for her. Cisco's nickname of *El Gato* was well deserved, which was the very reason most law enforcement types used it, but hated it. Many stories had popped up in the national press over the years that *El Gato* had been killed or captured. He had been surrounded in his villa in Mexico City, or caught at a border check point disguised as an old man. Each time he slipped away or the facts had been incorrect.

El Gato's run to the top of the cartel had been ruthless. A quiet man, he sat back and observed the habits and weaknesses of his superiors. When the time was right, he never hesitated to kill them. With Sonny's direction, Elena had worked her way higher and higher in the cartel until the number one man took notice of her extreme beauty.

She was magazine-cover beautiful, cunning and wicked smart. At her core, she had an insatiable Jones for adventure. Other female undercover informants Sonny had worked with had simply traded out their bodies to gain traction. Not Elena, she was too smart and too beautiful for that. Sonny had a theory about her magic and how she worked it, after watching her in action these last two years. Her beauty was so disarming to the average guy, that once she planted the idea that she might have an interest in him, his mind would go numb. She was then able to put these men into a form of suspended animation while she emptied their brains and contact lists. Sonny had seen this work on the toughest of bad guys.

A loud horn from an oncoming VW beetle snapped Sonny out of his wonderland and he regained control of the vehicle. The crumpled piece of paper with the address lay on the seat beside him. He had to get there before *El Gato* took Elena to another safe house.

The adobe wall was unmanned and the gate looked to be protected only by an old, wrought-iron fence. Made sense, Sonny thought. No one knew this was one of *El Gato's* safe houses yet. They wouldn't be expecting him at night anyway. Sonny glanced at the digital dash clock flashing 10:45. These days anybody out past the Reynosa city curfew of 8 p.m. had to be either a professional killer or a load runner for one of the cartels. It had become much too dangerous for regular folk and even experienced DEA agents. Sonny stopped the SUV, a few feet from the gate and dropped it into low. He eased the Detroit beast over the low curb and punched the accelerator. The black luxury tank flattened the gate and roared into the empty courtyard. Sonny saw a flash of fire as his headlights caught a man running and firing a pistol toward him. Sonny gunned it, causing the Cadillac to fishtail in a circle covering the courtyard in a cloud of dust. A bullet crashed through the windshield and shattered Sonny's rear view mirror.

"Dammit," Sonny screamed.

The gunman popped up in front of him. Sonny jerked the wheel hard right and his front bumper grazed the man's pant leg and jacket. The man ran up onto a front porch, holstered his pistol, pulled out a fresh one and began firing again. Sonny sped by quickly, leaning low against his door to avoid being shot. At the end of the courtyard, Sonny spun the truck around, letting the dust cloud clear just a little. With the headlights reflecting in every direction, being inside that cloud was like being on a carnival ride.

Sonny could see that the bad guy wanted to play. The gunman cleared the end of the porch on the run, firing his new weapon at the Escalade while running for the safety of the other porch across the way. Sonny was ready this time. He punched the accelerator while he used his left arm to fire his nine millimeter out the window at the gunman. Sonny saw him go down, blood saturating his white pant leg from the bullet hole. The 5,500-lb. monster rolled over the gunman like he was a twig.

"Gawddammit," Sonny yelled. "You better fuckin' be alive." He was pissed at himself mostly. Keeping the vehicle between him and the big house, he stepped out of it. He looked down at the shooter who was now in pieces. Blood pumped from an active, torn artery in his left arm. His right arm had been crushed and his left foot was up near his ear, which hung by a bloody tendon. The shooter looked up at Sonny.

"Kill me...please. Don't leave me," the shooter begged in Spanish.

"I'll do you that favor *paisano*, right after you tell me where El Jefe has taken Elena, my heart." The mangled man wheezed, coughed and spit out more blood but managed to speak.

"He-he, you...you won't find her. They go....Estados Unidos"

"My compliments to *El Diablo*," Sonny said. He raised his shaking gun and paid off his part of the deal.

Ben Riggs wore his Texas Sheriff's shirt out over his starched jeans. His cowboy boots made no sound as he crossed the length of the empty Hidalgo County Sheriffs office. At six-foot-two and two hundred eighty pounds he moved more like a quarterback than a linebacker. The recent election had made Ben, at thirty two, the youngest Sheriff in county history. His dark features were often mistaken for those of a *Latino* but, in reality, Ben like Elena was an American Indian.

"Junior? Braden? Where the hell is everybody?" the sheriff called out. He passed a ringing phone atop a cluttered desk as he made his way past four other desks in an open bullpen area.

"I miss the vacation memo?" he called out loudly again to himself. Ben unlocked his office door to the sound of his phone ringing. He crossed the floor in two steps, and then rummaged around his overwhelmed desktop from the visitor's side. The sheriff found the offensive phone underneath an open newspaper.

"*Ta Ueno*," Sheriff Riggs answered.

"Thank God I caught you, Sheriff. Randall Bates here, I'm the SAC here at Justice in D.C. How's business down your way?"

"Boomin,' Agent Bates. How can we help?"

"Call me Randall, please, Sheriff, I've heard great things about how you and your men have been handling the exploding violence down that way." There was a pause where agent Bates expected a thank you, or at least some commiseration from Sheriff Ben.

"I got a lot goin' on, Agent Bates. What can I do for you, specifically?" Ben asked.

"Ahh, yeah, sure. I've got four men that will be arriving first thing in the morning on special assignment. I'd greatly appreciate it if you could kind of point 'em in the right direction. Geographically speaking, of course," Agent Bates said.

"We will, of course, accommodate them any way we can. I thought the DEA handled all of Justice's dirty work?"

"Ha. Normally that's true. What the hell. I shouldn't share this outside departmental channels, Sheriff, but you need to know that you and your men are in the path of an incoming shit storm."

"Really?" Sheriff Ben Riggs asked.

"We have a deep-cover C.I. near the top of the Gulf cartel's leadership. We expect that one Cisco Ruiz, this, this, *El Gato* character, will be crossing into these United States. I don't have to tell you what a live capture of a cartel leader of this magnit..." The line went dead.

Sheriff Ben was already at his gun case where he had grabbed a box of ammo and a rifle. Slipping the rifle strap over his shoulder, he stormed out his office door. A deputy stood at a desk, talking on the phone that had been ringing earlier. He turned his gaze on the Sheriff as he spoke to the caller.

"No Ma'am, cows are not a priority...we will check on it though," the deputy said and hung up the phone.

"Where ya headed, Sheriff?"

"Got word," the Sheriff said over his shoulder, "*El Gato* is headed our way." The deputy, who had now fallen in behind Ben, winced noticeably.

"Well, ah Sheriff, Braden's already got Elena's mom's place staked out." Sheriff Ben stopped short and turned to eye the lean, young deputy.

"Just what is it you boys forgot to tell me?" Ben asked.

"We spotted two of *El Gato's* men hangin' round town couple'a days ago." Ben turned and was back in high gear as the deputy worked to keep pace. The deputy continued.

"Junior and Braden been takin' shifts watchin' Elena's mom's place. You know the one you set up for her. Braden just thought, why get you all rile...I mean involved, ya know, less somethin' really happens." The deputy stopped just in time to miss being hit by the swinging glass double doors as Ben hurried outside.

Ben was almost to his truck when a clean-cut guy in a brown, J.C. Penney suit stepped up to him and flipped open his badge.

"Stevens, DEA." Ben reached around Stevens and opened the door on his Hidalgo County Sheriff's Chevy Tahoe, as Stevens kept talking.

"I'm the new division head over in Laredo. Just took ov..." Ben cut him off.

"Know who you are, Stevens. Just shocked they let you wear that suit," Ben said as he slid the rifle over to the passenger seat.

"Look, Sheriff, we are not your enemy on this. It's best for everyone's safety if we know where you have secreted Maria Sampedro, Elena's mother. She's going to need Federal protection. A few worn out cowboys won't be enough."

"Your agency has more leaks in it than the Mexican *Policia*. Maria Sampedro is in the protective custody of Hidalgo County. You'll excuse me, we got cows loose out on the Baxter ranch. Big, expensive cows." He smiled and brushed by Stevens as he opened the door to his Tahoe wider and got in. Stevens shut the door for him and rested his arm on the truck's open window.

"I know all about Elena being your main squeeze, Sheriff. I feel for you, hell...we all do. But high school is over," Stevens said.

"You drive all the way out here to lecture me on teen romance?" Ben asked.

"Fraid not. One of our boys has gone rogue. He shows up, just know he's not acting on behalf of the agency," Stevens said.

"Sonny Calderone?" Ben said.

"How'd you know that?" Stevens asked.

"Hell, if you boys had control of your agents, Elena wouldn't be in this mess." Ben started the Tahoe, put it in reverse and backed up slowly. Stevens kept talking.

"What is it? Her hold on men? Magic, ya think?" Stevens yelled out. Ben just looked at him and shook his head. He dropped the shifter into drive and sped away.

Ben sensed something was wrong as he pulled up to the trailer. Braden's Tahoe was parked in the yard with the driver's front door open. Ben drew his service revolver and walked up to the truck carefully. The key was in the ignition and the police radio had been blasted to pieces, probably by a shotgun. No sign of Braden. Ben eased past the chickens pecking in the front yard and stepped up onto the deck. The front door showed no sign of damage. He looked through the glass into the living room. Nothing was out of place. Family photos were still propped on end tables and covered the kitchen coffee bar that joined the two rooms together.

"Braden?" Ben called out, as he scanned the kitchen through the glass.

"Maria? Maria Sampedro?" Ben opened the door and led with his forty-five. No obvious sign of a struggle. A box of Russell Stover assorted candies sat next to a stack of old family photos on the coffee bar. There was one of Elena as a young school girl. Even then she had a presence. Elena at sixteen, laughing, while hanging on to a young, long-haired Ben Riggs' as he steered his motorcycle. Her glowing brown skin and hair made the camera search her out. Those qualities along with her bright, perfect white teeth made her stand out no matter who else was in the picture. Three separate, framed 8 x10 pictures showed Elena smiling from the cover of fashion magazines. Ben moved away from the memories and down the hall.

"Braden?" Ben heard something and threw open the hall closet door. There was Braden, bound and gagged, folded up like an accordion. At first, Ben thought he was dead but, as the light hit

Braden's pleading eyes, Ben breathed easier. Ben removed the gag and started on the hand restraints.

"Elena saved my life. Thank God it's you, Ben. I thought one of the bodyguards had come back to finish me off."

Ben slowed when he touched a bloody bandage on Braden's right hand.

"Eww, damn that hurts. Just a flesh wound though. She's still a great shot. Ben." Ben helped Braden to stand, then, walked him to the couch so he could stretch and let the blood return to his legs.

"What the hell happened?" Ben asked.

"They forced Maria to signal me and that brought me down from my post. Soon as I was in the door, one of *El Gato's* goons jumped me and I was good as dead. Elena grabbed a pistol from *El Gato's* waist band and saved me."

"Saved you? Looks like she shot an officer and interfered with an active investigation," Ben said.

"I know what you're doing Ben...don't," Braden said.

"Elena bandage your hand then?" Ben asked. Braden smiled, nodding his head up and down.

"He had Elena. Why come for her mom?" Ben asked

"Had a Catholic priest too. Elena promised to marry the

desperado, but only in the U.S.," Braden said.

Ben kicked a coffee table into the wall, and then crushed the box of candy on the counter with his fist as he stared out the window into the vast, empty South Texas landscape. For the first time today, Ben felt defeated. Braden shook him out of it.

"Only reason I'm alive is that Elena threatened to call off the wedding if he let his men kill me. She may be his hostage but, you know Elena, she's in charge."

"We've got no idea where they're headed," Ben said. He started to pace in front of the couch. "It'll have to be someplace where his men can get him back across the river to safety."

"I never knew Elena was so sentimental." Braden said.

"You're still losing blood let's get you to town to see Doc Rivers." Ben helped Braden up onto his feet. "Keep that hand straight up in the air," Sheriff Ben said.

"She kept repeating it. 'I want doves we can release, Irish doves.' And she looked right at me when she said it."

Ben pushed the door open and they stepped onto the deck, "Damn," Ben said. "You get yourself to the doc, okay?"

"Sure, why?"

"Doves are her signal. Las Palomas means the doves in

English. Las Palomas wildlife area. They can be across the Rio Grande safely into Mexico in no time from there," Ben said.

"But boss, there's three different Palomas wildlife areas."

"Irish doves must mean Kelly management area. Think about it, Braden, it's the closest to the bridge."

Sonny Calderone flashed his smile and his DEA badge at the Border Patrol check point on the Pharr Internacional Bridge and was back into these Estados Unidos without ever having to bring the black Escalade to a complete stop. The sun had just come up. The contrast of the filthy streets behind him and the manicured lawns of Hildago Texas he now rolled by had never before been so vivid.

Sonny felt he had come to a hyper-understanding of the world and where he and Elena fit into it. Sweat dripped from his face onto the glass of the framed 8x10 of him and Elena he held in front of him. Sonny nodded, his eyes closed for a second. He was jolted back to reality with a noise and the sight of the rear end of the eighteen-wheeler in front of him. He stood on the brake hard and power-gripped the wheel, willing the SUV to stop. The truck slid to within a quarter of an inch of the eighteen-wheeler's rear steel safety bar.

"Sunovabitch," Sonny screamed. He laid on his horn as if that would make the truck move. Wide awake now, he fumed impatiently as the semi edged forward four or five inches. Sonny's nerves were ragged and he knew the miracle effects of the white powder had worn off. He cranked the steering wheel hard left and pushed the Caddy out into oncoming traffic. The first oncoming trucker reacted in shock and jackknifed his rig into the ditch. The second managed to swerve onto and ride the shoulder until the mad man had passed. Sonny roared past the constipated line of semis and cut back into his lane. Ten blocks up, he turned left out of the residential area and onto a street lined with factories. Sonny coasted in behind a parked car and cut the engine. He pulled his portable police radio from its hiding place under the dash, switched it on, and then spun the dial to three. Static.

Sonny grabbed the empty liquor bottle. Taking his radio, Sonny exited and went to the rear tailgate door and opened it. He laid the radio down and wrestled with a box marked Cuervo Gold Tequila. Finally, he got the box to the edge and ripped the cardboard top off. He pulled out a fresh bottle, ripped the lid off, turned the bottle up and took a powerful pull before he brought it down to eye level.

"Eye, eye, eye, whoop, whoop. I'm seeing you, you, little

gusano sonovabitch." Sonny gave the little worm in the bottle his meanest look. The radio squawked to life.

"We are 10-33 channels to 10-57," a woman's voice squawked out in even tones. Probably a dispatcher. Sonny pulled a silver cigarette case from the tequila box and popped it open. It held an overflow of white powder, complete with crystalline gleaming rocks and a silver straw. Sonny put the straw to work and took a break only after the case was nearly empty. He spun around, tossed the empty tequila bottle into the air, whipped out his Glock and shattered the bottle with one shot.

"I'm coming for you, Elena. I am coming to save you, Baby." Sonny knew "33" was emergency radio traffic meaning they were switching channels. "57" meant a request for back up, but what channel had they gone to? He was proud of one thing. He alone was the reason the Sheriff had gone to another channel, of that Sonny was certain. He pocketed the cigarette case, grabbed the radio and the three quarters-full bottle of Gold and got back behind the wheel. He turned the police radio from three on upward, not really stopping at any channel. Then it hit him. The Geological Survey Channel, it was the only one that could be open for traffic. Sonny tuned in Channel 12 just in time to hear a familiar voice.

"Requesting 10-57 (back up) for 10-56 (meeting at) Las Palomas, Kelly area. Signal 32 (kidnapping) by a signal 29-F (wanted felon)," Sheriff Ben's voice rang out over the radio. Sonny picked up the framed 8x10 and smiled at how beautiful Elena looked. He brought the picture to his lips and kissed it.

Ben looked through the rifle scope at the scene below. One of *El Gato's* goons had just finished ripping out low lying bushes from a flat area overlooking the Rio Grande River. This would be the place. Ben had managed to find a rocky spot overlooking it all. Unlike most of South Texas, the Las Palomas was loaded with vegetation and trees. It was so lush and tropical looking that movie crews had used it more than once to double as a jungle. Ben had caught a glimpse of the wedding party earlier but they were currently out of sight. The group was made up of the groom, Cisco Ruiz (*El Gato*), the bride, Elena Sampedro, nee Ruiz, Elena's mom, Maria, the Mexican priest and the two ugliest bodyguards Ben had seen in his fourteen years in law enforcement. Braden had described the two as a Mad Mr. Clean and Manson and Ben could not disagree. The goons both held a long bulky mystery beneath their jackets.

Ben's attention was diverted by the sound of people partying. He pulled the scope up and saw that a gang of about twenty cartel members had gathered for the ceremony across the river in Mexico. This was a real wild card because the river was so narrow at this point that they would be able to fire and hit someone on the U.S. side. They were the madman's insurance policy back to safety, no doubt. *El Gato* stepped into the clearing followed by Elena and the others. Ben was surprised by the sight of a seventh person. Small of stature and gaunt, it could only be Elena's eighty-seven-year old grandpa, *Don Miguel.* Sure, someone to give Elena away. She would have insisted on *Don Miguel.* She had always been the old man's favorite grandchild. He had retired from the railroad years ago but his real job was that of the tribe's medicine man. He was ancient now but still a man of great personal power. Ben knew now that even if his back up were late getting to the wedding, the odds had just shifted back to the good guys.

"Don't fuckin' breathe, *gringo.*" Ben felt cold metal dig into his neck.

"Hey friend...just doin' some deer hunting," Ben said. He eased up off his rock with the gun pressed against his back. A rookie fuckin' mistake. He had gotten so wrapped up in saving Elena he had gone forward on an assumption. He acted on what Braden had seen and took that as a known number of goons when clearly the number was unknown. Manson and Mr. Clean had back up. The two men pulled Ben up onto his feet and snatched his rifle. Ben looked the two of them over. Had to be Dumb and Dumber he thought. Dumb dropped the rifle off of Ben's upper back finally but Dumber pointed a pistol at Ben's temple and cocked it.

"Carlos, *El Jefe* say no keel peoples, hee's wedding."

"Ees a feeckin' *Federale*," Dumber insisted. "We keel *Federales*." Dumb circled behind Sheriff Ben, who figured on buying some time.

"Hell, I'm just county sheriff, this ain't n..." An axe handle exploded into the back of Ben's head. Ben went down...and out.

The big bass drum in Ben's head had a thousand tambourines attached to it and, with every beat; the tambourines rang out like a hundred surgeons banging a scalpel of pain into brain tissue. The sound was overwhelming and the drumbeats were getting closer together. One of Ben's eyes popped open involuntarily. Elena's bottom, clothed in a fine white dress in front of him was unmistakably real. The desperate tenor of it all quickly came scrambling back to him. He could hear the priest chanting in Latin. Ben took control and forced his other eye open. The pounding in the back of his head was so painful and distracting he had to wall it off to have any chance of survival.

Ben found himself strapped tightly into a wooden folding chair, the one and only front-row witness to the travesty of a lifetime. A rag was stuffed into his mouth. His arms had been forced over the back of the chair where his hands were bound tightly together. He couldn't turn his head because any move caused the ropes to tear deeper into his wrists, but Dumb and Dumber must be standing guard behind him. He didn't have to see it to know that the object that poked into his back was the business end of a rifle. Relief washed over Ben as he could hear from the conversation that the wedding had not yet taken place. Saving Elena and her family was job one, but Elena was Catholic. It was important for that reason if not a whole lot more reasons that Elena leave here a single woman. Mr. Clean and Manson stood watching their boss while *El Gato* argued with his future bride about Ben's treatment.

"He's a guest, what more do you want?" *El Gato* asked.

"Let me loosen the ropes," Elena pleaded.

She ambled over to Ben's chair as if she had won the

argument. *El Gato* protested, and then stopped short.

"Okay, okay," *El Gato* said.

Elena wasted no time. She leaned over Ben and kissed him on the cheek. She pulled the rag from his mouth and tossed it at Manson. She carefully poured water into his mouth from her water bottle.

"I'm sorry, Baby," Elena purred at Ben. He said nothing, so as not to alert the assholes to what Elena had done. She took her time, making over him and continuing to peck him on both cheeks and once on the lips. She scooted his chair a bit which caused Dumb to spring into action. Finally Ben had a read on where he was posted. While Dumb scooted Ben and the chair to where she had instructed, Elena fussed with his hand restraints. Ben felt the blood rush back into his hands again. Dumb plopped Ben's chair down. Now, at least, he was closer to the ceremony.

"C'mon Elena, we got to start," Cisco said.

"Music! You promised me music," Elena demanded.

"Music is here, Honey. Let's go." A lone Mexican dressed in black and carrying an accordion was being hustled down the pathway by Dumber. Good, all bad guys accounted for.

El Gato looked handsome in his white tux, Ben thought. Cisco

Ruiz was actually a good looking man. Women would likely say he was tall, dark and handsome. Most killers had a face to match their horrible karma. Not this guy. The dapper groom stood facing the priest and the Rio Grande and he kept twisting his head over his right shoulder to catch a glimpse of the bride. Manson and Mr. Clean stood on either side of him. They had changed into red tuxedo jackets, bulky hidden guns included and they looked every bit the groomsmen. The man on the accordion stood off to Ben's left, playing an old Mexican folk song. Ben was now able to turn his head and see Elena marching toward them, her arm linked with that of her grandpa, *Don Miguel*. The old medicine man was steady on his feet, but slow. Ben worked the razor blade slowly back and forth against his rope restraints so as not to alert the guards. He was grateful to Elena for slipping it to him but it was an old safety razor blade with dual sharp edges. With every stroke one side of the blade cut into his hand. As Elena and *Don Miguel* marched closer, Ben began to wonder where the hell law enforcement was. Border patrol would have picked up this many people gathered on both sides of the river on their ground sensors. Failing that, their new surveillance drone would've spotted them and scheduled a look-see. DEA had someone inside this little party, so they damn well knew Ruiz was inside the United States. Bates, Randall Bates called from Justice to say they were sending four men tomor... YES, tomorrow. AFTER Ruiz was safely back home in Mexico, not today. Ben sure as hell hoped Junior could round up Victor like he had left word for him to do. His call for back up otherwise would be purposely ignored. This afternoon of peace, Ben now realized, had been bought and paid for by Ruiz, from Justice all the way down. Elena and *Don Miguel* marched by Ben.

"Stop that music," a voice screamed out from behind them. The accordion player kept smiling and playing. A bullet ripped through his out-stretched instrument and dropped him to the dirt. The accordion let out one last, long, tuneless note.

"Elena, move away," Sonny Calderone yelled. "I don't want you to get hurt." Sonny stood in the open like a gunfighter, a pistol in each hand. What an idiot. Ben slumped lower in his chair.

"Sonny, don't," Elena screamed.

Sonny started firing. Elena, Maria and *Don Miguel* hit the dirt. The priest, used to life in a Mexican border town, also dropped flat to the ground right where he was. Dumber fell into Ben's lap and slid to the ground leaking blood. Mr. Clean and Manson had pushed in front of *El Gato* as soon as trouble arrived. The bulk underneath their jackets turned out to be sub machine guns clipped to shoulder slings. They calmly, professionally and in unison raised the two automatic weapons and fired. A spray of twenty rounds each burst forth like laser guided missiles. Sonny was rocked backward as bloody holes blasted open up and down his body. He was killed instantly. Dumb had been hit in the leg by one of Sonny's bullets and was hopping around screaming in pain. Dumber had taken one in the head and lay dead at Ben's feet. Ben worked feverishly raking the razor against the thick ropes that bound his hands. Elena sat on the ground crying, her white dress now dirty. Grandpa *Don Miguel* and Maria did their best to comfort her. She had not been hit, Ben was sure of that. He was also sure now that *El Gato's* two guards were using PS90's, automatic sub-machine guns like the Secret Service used. Preferred by professionals on both sides of the law, they easily penetrated body armor. The Kevlar vest Ben sweated under would offer no advantage. Ruiz, the upset groom, rushed to Elena and helped her up.

"You okay, Baby? Tell me you're okay," he said.

"I'll make it," she said. "Help Poppy, he's old." Ben felt the last of the rope threads binding his hands behind his back give way. He eyed Manson who walked toward them. Mr. Clean was busy rendering aid to Dumb. Ben squeezed his hands together so the rope wouldn't drop to the ground and give him away. *El Gato* bent down, propped his hands under *Don Miguel's* arms and got him on his feet. Ben watched closely. The old man looked into Ruiz's eyes as if he wanted to tell him something. This drew *El Gato* in. *Don Miguel* flattened out his open palm and quickly blew white powder into *El Gato's* face. Ben checked the guards. Not one of them had caught it. *El Gato* bent and hugged *Don Miguel*. The old man looked him in the eye and spoke to him forcefully. Ben was too far away to hear what was said. Elena slipped her arm around the old man and kissed him on the cheek.

El Gato turned toward his men.

"Gather your things and go home. Share my message with all you see. I am a man of peace."

"You okay here, *El Jefe*?" Manson asked. Mr. Clean joined the group and circled around *El Gato* looking him over from head to toe.

"This a joke, *El Jefe*?" Mr. Clean asked his boss. Ben eyed Dumber's pistol which lay just outside the reach of his foot. He knew *Don Miguel* had ended the prospect of the wedding and now it was up to him to see that Elena and family lived to celebrate. Ben figured *Don Miguel*'s special powder, whatever it was, would soon wear off. The cartel boss could snap out of it at any minute. With Dumb to his left, wounded and moaning and the other two guards just a few feet from him, he considered his options. If he took out Manson and Mr. Clean first, Dumb would have too much time to react. If Dumb were shot first, Ben would be exposed to bursts of automatic PS90 fire. The question was; how many rounds did the gun at his feet hold? No time to plan. Ben rose up, and dived for the gun on the ground. Dumb was already reaching for his forty-five. Ben pointed the gun at Dumb but he could tell it was too light. The ammo clip was gone. In one motion Ben hurled the handgun at Dumb's head, picked up his chair and swung it at Manson who was running toward him. Mr. Clean had moved into position protecting his boss with his body while pulling his PS90 up ready for action. The chair slammed into Manson's knees and he started to go down. In a flash Ben grabbed Manson's body and twisted him into position as a shield while he pulled Manson's sub-machine gun up ready to fire. Mr. Clean had his finger on the trigger of his PS90 and it was pointed at Ben. Ben couldn't shoot without hitting Elena and her family. *El Gato* put his hand on Mr. Clean's gun barrel.

"Stop the violence," *El Gato* yelled. He walked over to Ben, who had Manson in a head lock. He looked into Manson's face. "Stop resisting, he will let you go." Instinctively, Manson relaxed. Ben released the hold on his head but still gripped his shoulder. *El Gato* pointed at Dumb who had been knocked out by Ben's pitch. "Pick up your brother; carry him across the Rio Bravo." Manson stared at him in disbelief. "Go now," *El Gato* said in a loud voice. "You will be the rock on which I build my church."

"You must go too, my son," *El Gato* said as he pointed at Mr. Clean. Something about the conviction in his tone seemed real to Ben. Looking around he saw that the Catholic priest was already in the river wading home. *El Gato* had an arm around each of his two remaining goons and was walking them back to the bluff where a few seconds ago his wedding had been about to happen. Dumb was across Manson's shoulder. Out cold.

"Fear not. My protection is from above," El Gato said. "Go back to my people and tell them what you have seen." He moved his arm down their backs and gave them each a gentle push. They turned to stare at him in disbelief but said nothing as they too started down the hill to the river. Ben relaxed a little. Elena rushed over and threw her arms around him. The gang across the river were yelling and cheering the returning men, thinking that the wedding was over. Ben could remember hearing about a very special potion as a young boy on the reservation. The elders told a story of how many years ago a terrible war had broken out between two tribes. The war had killed many young warriors and peace could not be found. Their chief had gone to the tribe's medicine man begging him for help. The powerful man told his leader that he could end the war immediately with this special powder but, once used on a man, that man's free will would be gone forever. The medicine man did as instructed and blew the powder into the face of the opposing tribe's chief. Once inhaled, his entire will was given over to the medicine man, which had him demand peace from his tribesmen. Peace became everlasting between the two warring tribes.

This was a powder made from three plants whose recipe was known only to a select few men of tremendous personal power. The concoction held the power of life itself because when used on a person, that person's free will, their very persona was history forever. There was no antidote. In keeping with those like Don

Miguel whose purpose was focused on the practice of good medicine, not bad, the powder was rarely if ever used. If the potent powder was used at all it was to be only as a final option. This eternal solution had to be what *Don Miguel* had been forced to use to save his granddaughter. Ben picked up the pistol from the ground and tucked it in his belt.

"You can put all those away. He won't be any trouble," *Don Miguel* said. Maria smiled at *Don Miguel.*

"Bless you, Poppy," Maria said as she hugged her dad. *El Gato* walked back to them now. He took Elena's free hand and joined it with Ben's. He had the most radiant smile anyone had ever seen. Ben could see his men and a platoon of other law enforcement agency types hurrying up the path toward them now. "You'll need to go with these men, Cisco." Ben told him.

"Thank you for calling me by my real name," Cisco Ruiz said as he beamed at them. *Don Miguel* told Cisco to place his hands in front of him and Ben snapped on the handcuffs. Elena turned to Ben. She smiled, he leaned toward her and she threw her arms around him. Ben hugged her like he would never let go. Elena kissed his ear and whispered.

"I knew you'd come for me." Ben held her out at arm's length and looked into her eyes.

"I'm just that easy for you, huh?" he said.

"No, Ben. Not like that. You're the world to me. When we were about to die I could only think of one thing...." Ben pressed his index finger against Elena's lips then followed up with his lips, for a long, long time.

Maybe the arriving men were surprised to see one of the world's most ruthless killers suddenly become a meek, peaceful man. Maybe they were shocked when Cisco Ruiz said he planned to tell law enforcement all about his 'other life' and where a hundred and fifty million dollars had been stashed. Ben couldn't be sure, because he and Elena were in the woods rediscovering their love and discussing why, in this life, first love is the one that cuts the deepest.

Céline

Céline was bored with life and she was sure that her next great adventure was about to come along and rescue her. She liked to sit in the sand down by the Santa Monica pier and focus on the farthest wave in the ocean out on the distant horizon. Céline had plans for that wave. But I didn't know any of this then. I was aware of only one truth. Céline was the most sensuous, beautiful blond to ever walk this earth. Her appeal was compounded by her soft feather-bed voice and her sexy French accent. Believe me, it took some time and more than a little work to get her to consider using her sultry voice to speak that French to me. Once I had won her over I wasted no time. I insisted that she give me lessons in French. Her pouty lips actually took on the shape of a heart when she slowed to enunciate the French oo's and eww's for me.

"*Oeuf* like oof en Engles. Zee, look at ze leeeps. Ooof or uhf," she said.

"I see how you do it. It just doesn't come out right when I say it," I told her. "I remember what it means though. Eggs," I said proudly. Céline smirked and quickly pricked my balloon of confidence.

"It means egg. Eggs would be *oeufs*. I love it, you are so goofy," Céline said as she squeezed my cheeks together with her thumb and forefinger. Céline was now speaking English with a hint of a French accent. She created a sound and a tone with her voice that could melt ammunition. She moved seamlessly between French, English and French-accented English. The latter she used mostly on men, especially when she wanted something from them. She had another rough, guttural German dialect I had yet to hear. It was spoken only for work.

I was over-spending my way through law school, so I was driving a cab on the L.A. night shift. About three times a week the dispatcher would call out a fare for pickup at the Beverly Hilton hotel on Wilshire. The call was for a guest of the hotel, Céline.

Sometimes when I've had too much to drink, I wonder what type of law clients I would be working with had Céline not gotten into my cab that first night. It does no good to rearrange the past in your mind though. What I do know is, the moment the blonde angel in a willowy, white cotton dress slid into the back seat of my cab, my life changed forever. Given the chance now I would not go back and change a thing. From that moment on I had to possess her. She would be mine, no matter the cost. Money had never really motivated me, but if I needed to become wealthy to have her, so be it.

Her destination was usually a different mansion, always in Bel Air, Beverly Hills or the Hollywood Hills. She carried a huge leather YSL bag which looked heavy, the zipper stretched as taught as a clothesline in a tornado.

"You married?" I asked.

"Do I fuckin' look married?" she snapped. I adjusted the rear view mirror to look at her eyes and settled for her sunglasses.

"There's a Rare Earth cafe, just opened in Westwood. Best avocado salad in the world, you'll love it," I said. Céline uncrossed her legs, shifted closer to the door and muttered something in French.

"What was that?" I asked.

"You can't afford me," Céline said. "Just give it up."

"You don't know, I could be a super billionaire, who drives a hack to meet hot women," I said.

"Turn up here," she said.

I protested, "I know my way up the hill and this is not th..." Céline cut me off.

"Turn," she screamed. I swung across a lane of traffic at the last minute and made the turn.

"You a newbie or just a fuck up?" Céline asked.

"I am anything you want me to be," I told her. Céline shook her head from side to side. I stared at her in the rear view mirror for too long and had to jerk the wheel hard right to narrowly avoid a row of parked cars on the cramped hillside street.

"Damn...wild man," she said.

"You'll go with me then?" I asked. Céline grabbed the back of my seat and pulled herself forward 'til her lips were touching my ear.

"Up here, on the left," she whispered. "See the black wrought-iron gate?" Her scent filled my nostrils and drove a longing deep into my solar plexus. Céline bit into my earlobe, and then languorously leaned back.

I stopped the cab in the apron of the driveway, the front bumper almost touching the large black security gate. Céline read from my city license posted on the front dashboard.

"So, Billy Billionaire is Nick Adams today?" Before I could answer, she exited the back seat and stood at my open window. She reached in, dropped a Benjamin in my lap and turned toward the gate. I hurried out my door and caught her just as she pushed the button on the intercom. A man answered.

"That you, Baby?"

"Don't ever address me in that manner...peon," Céline barked. Her German accent and gruff manner startled me, this being the first time I heard it. I stood just behind her, frozen. A wad of ones and fives peeked out of my fist. The gate buzzed and then started to swing open. Céline seemed to suddenly realize I was there as she started up the long driveway.

"What now?" she asked in her natural, soft, sexy voice.

"Your change."

"That's your tip, *imbécile*," she laughed. I just stared at her, entranced by her remarkable beauty.

"Drive away now and I'll ask for you by name next time," she said firmly. That was just the enticement I needed. I turned back toward my cab.

"Yeah, I mean thanks." I turned back around and walked backward watching her perfectly rounded bottom as she made the climb up the steep driveway. Céline raised her hand over her shoulder and waved, never turning around. I managed to get back outside the gate just as it slammed shut. I had caught just a brief glimpse of the monument to capitalism perched at the top of the driveway. I could just imagine a top-of-the-Hollywood-hills view that was spectacular. The mansion's opulence made me wonder what service Céline could be offering this real-life billionaire.

When I next got her call, I learned Céline had come to the City of Angels as a model-actress but soon discovered she much preferred being the one doing the directing. By chance she happened upon a closely held secret. Many of the most powerful men in Los Angeles enjoyed nothing better than being dominated and punched around by a beautiful woman. Lose $200 million of your studio's money on a sure-shot Mike Myers comedy? Take your punishment. Lose a billion of your bank's money on credit default swaps? You've got to pay up, somehow. Céline was their mistress of collection, their master of pain. Whether it was speed-balling oranges into their nut sack or tying them up and punishing them for their hits and misses with whips and chains, Céline was strictly professional. Sex was not allowed. Clients were never permitted to touch her sexually, or in any way. They could, however, count on her discretion. Céline's fee was deposited electronically into her bank account 24 hours before her visit. Most clients, in addition, paid a very stiff monthly retainer to guarantee their spot. Any violation of her rules meant banishment from her client list. If the violation was flagrant enough, it also meant that the client referring the offender would also be dropped. These powerful men, whose money, prestige and power could command or buy allegiance from almost anyone, had a burning need to serve and an aching for release by a very beautiful woman. Céline happily was making a six figure income acting the part and dishing it out.

The first time we made love I memorized every second of the whole session. I didn't know at the time how badly I would need to hit the replay button over the next year. I had lived in L.A. for four years but it was only after I met Céline that I discovered what the city was all about. We spent time at the Griffith Observatory looking at the stars through the big 12 inch Zeiss telescope. We acted out scenes from *Rebel Without A Cause* on the grounds, in the same locations they had used for the movie. We liked to come back after dark and take pictures chasing each other around the grounds with the burst of the photo flash. We caught a glimpse of Natalie Wood and James Dean once, running up ahead but just out of our reach. Céline loved Catalina Island more than anywhere else in the world and I came to agree with her on that. At first we spent our weekend trips in a nice hotel in Avalon. We would rent one of the small jeeps they offered and drive up into the hills finding new places to explore among the Eucalyptus trees and the scrub brush. Sunday night always came too soon with threats of Monday's workaday world ready to pull us apart and fling us back into our very different jobs.

One glorious weekend, one of Céline's more generous clients offered us the use of his exclusive yacht which he kept anchored in the Avalon harbor. It came with full staff including a very fine chef. This was like entering a different world. While sunning ourselves on the deck one day, the topic turned to what it would be like to live like royalty full time. Céline had some very definite ideas about what things we would acquire first. Better still, an opportunity, a rare opportunity had recently presented itself. As for me, I was madly in love with a woman who exceeded my expectations in every way. In Céline, I had finally found my soul mate. We were a match on so many levels. I was the person I wanted to be when she was around. For the next four months, we spent all our free time together, making love and plotting....

I pushed my fake mustache up with my tongue and racked a round into the pump-action shotgun I held. The bald, portly, powerful, international banker in front of me did not, at this moment, look so powerful. He stood in the center of his opulent living room on his expensive Norwegian wood floor, wearing only his boxers. His little dick, still hard, was firmly in his grasp as it protruded out the front flap of his undies. Céline stood a few feet behind him in her leather boots, short leather skirt and leather bikini top. She held the handle of a bull whip, the studded tip still wrapped around his left leg. Bloody whip tracks marked his lower back and legs. His face was pocked with fear and anger.

"Who the hell are you?" he asked. I didn't answer; instead I circled to my left, still pointing the shotgun in front of me as I got a better look at his condition. I laughed hysterically.

"What the hell's going on here, Céline?" he asked, turning to face her head on.

"I've known you for three years. Half your damn clients are from me."

"Charlie, I'm just as scared as you are," Céline whispered innocently.

"Shut up, bitch," I yelled at Céline as I waved the gun at her. Charlie tried to tuck his deflated dick back into its barn stall. He turned his attention back to me and managed a weak smile.

"There's cash in the safe. Lots of cash you can hav..." I

smacked him in the face with the butt of my shotgun. He went down hard. Blood, saliva and teeth splattered onto the Norwegian wood.

"In that chair right behind him, bitch." I waved my weapon again at Céline, brushing it across her back when she didn't move fast enough. She plopped down in the chair and immediately slid to her knees and took Charlie's head in her hands. Tears rushed down her face.

"Why'd you have to hit him so hard?" she shrieked. "He was working with you."

Charlie looked up in complete shock. His lip was gashed open and he struggled for air as blood filled his mouth. Céline was off script but, as usual, her instincts were right. I roughly jerked her back up onto the chair and quickly rolled Charlie over face forward. He coughed up blood everywhere, but he was breathing. I dragged him out to the center of the room, dropped down and straddled him. I shoved the business end of the shotgun to the edge of his torn nostril.

Céline let out a scream. As most do in times of crisis, Charlie resorted to prayer. He muttered under his breath, which gave Céline an opening.

"Don't hurt him," she pleaded.

"What do you want?"

I pulled the barrel away from Charlie and pointed it toward her. I pulled the trigger, blasting the tall ceramic sculpture just to her left into a thousand little pieces. Céline sucked in air, too scared to speak now. If Charlie had doubts about her, we had just canceled them. I trained the shotgun back onto Charlie, who was still sobbing underneath me.

"Gawd, no," he said as he turned to cough out more blood.

"No need to call me God, just remember that's who I am," I told him before dropping the bomb.

"Your office safe, Fourteenth and Wilshire." I could see his eyes widen as he started to register the enormity of it all.

"No, no, they'll kill me."

"You don't tell me, I'll kill you.... Take your pick."

Charlie's eyes darted around the room as if his answer might be written on one of his well-appointed walls where his million dollar paintings hung.

"I can't, I can't, I'm telling you. You don't know these people. You don't understand," Charlie said.

"Seems to me your chances are better screwing them over,

cause you screw me and you are a dead man right now," I said, confident in my game. Céline was crying in fitful stops and starts.

"Please, Charlie, tell him. He damn near killed me just now. He's crazy."

I leaned forward and rested the barrel of the gun on Céline's lovely knee. I slid it up her leg past the edge of her black leather miniskirt.

"Don't you worry, Toots, I'm gonna see that you last a while," I said, sneering at her for effect. I felt something wet and warm under my foot.

"You fuck. I should kill you just for that." A puddle was forming on the floor by his boxers. He looked broken and started to sob like a little girl.

"Okay, okay. My heart is not good. Bring me pen and paper. I have to write it out, otherwise I can't remember all the numbers," Charlie said.

"You heard him, get it," I yelled at Céline. I took out my cell phone and pushed the number one as I cradled the shotgun under my arm. Céline scrambled up and ran to the kitchen. I turned my attention back to Charlie, trembling on the floor.

"I just signaled my partner who is now walking into your office building. When he calls back, I will hand you the phone. You will call out the numbers to him. Once he empties the safe, I'll walk away and you two can go back to your game." Céline handed Charlie the pen and paper. He placed it on the floor and wrote out several numbers.

"Lot a numbers I have to remember...ya know?"

"It's okay," I said. "The three of us will be right here together until my partner tells me he's clear."

"May take me a mi..." Charlie started to say.

"No," I yelled. "You try and juke us or signal somebody at your office and I will tune you up all over this high-dollar pad of yours. Then, when you think you can't take the pain anymore, I will shove this shotgun up your ass and pull the trigger. Leaves one hell of a mess." The phone rang.

Of course my only partner was Céline. Charlie was speaking to a recording. Once inside his office, I did not want to have to rely on just my memory. Céline had already given me the two keys I would need to access the elevator and enter his office. I injected our banker with a fast-acting sedative and I was almost ready to take off for his office and our payday. First came the part I dreaded most. Céline could not come out of this looking as beautiful as ever. I slapped her hard, once on each side of her face. After she insisted it wasn't enough, I finally punched her, causing her to lose consciousness for a bit. This upset me a lot more than it did her. I could tell it had worked though, as the skin around her left eye was already plumping up and, by morning, she would have a nice black shiner. Finally, I left for Charlie's office, my perfect future with Céline in sight. This was after kissing Céline on her owees and confirming our meet location for six months down the road.

Céline had masterminded this plan when she'd overheard a drunken Charlie discussing the extra quarter point he and his European bank contact were loading onto the latest international bailout. We tagged his phones and, after six weeks, we had all the details. They spoke in code but, from what the tap picked up, we expected a haul of just over one million dollars.

We had it all planned down to the penny. Céline, by staying behind, could make sure Charlie didn't wake up too soon and spoil our plans. Once the professional fugitive hunters came after me, she could stay close and keep an eye on their progress. The nice thing about stealing stolen money is you don't have to worry about the cops. If these hoodlums catch you though, you can count on a long, slow torture before they finish you off in the most painful way possible.

I walked out of the office with ten million dollars in Bearer bonds. Evidently, their little scam had worked a lot better than even they had imagined. Charlie had bought into Céline's act so strongly that he held firm in his support of her innocence. His partners, being more practical than sentimental, sweated her hard anyway. Céline held firm and did not break. This left her stuck in L.A. carrying on with her routine as if nothing had changed. It took them three days to ID me and, by then, I was four countries and six identities away. I knew all of this because of the letter relay system we had set up before I left. Céline had gotten her mom involved by telling her that I was a guy she was in love with who was still trying to get out of his bad marriage. Céline always wrote to her mom regularly, anyway. If the letter addressed to her mom had a certain stamp on it, her mom knew that instead of opening it, she was to drop it inside a larger envelope which had been pre-addressed to a drop box in Europe. The drop box owners would then forward that envelope to whatever address I provided them. I could change the address simply by calling a phone number they provided and entering the new forwarding address on the keypad. The system worked great and I was able to keep up with developing events back home, usually about a month behind their actual occurrence.

The heat was more intense than we had planned on. Probably owing to the fact that our haul was ten times what we had expected it to be. Céline was watched constantly and there was no way we could take a chance on meeting for at least a year. I dumped her half of the proceeds into her Swiss account when I was there to open up mine. In typical Céline fashion, she had maintained a private Swiss account since turning twenty-one. I hid out in Jamaica for awhile, but you really stick out down there when you have money. After touring France and England, I settled into life in a small, but prosperous, Dutch town just twenty kilometers outside Amsterdam. There I was free to be as big a conspicuous consumer as I wanted to be. Posing as a big time U.S. record producer, I lavished my dates with expensive gifts and big girl toys. Now with unlimited funds, I dated the most beautiful women in the world...and cared for none of them.

Céline was my constant mental companion. I replayed our first lovemaking session over and over along with mental trailers of every time we had touched. I was love sick. I was determined not to be undone though by what bounty hunters call the 3M's.

Anyone who hunts fugitives knows that keeping a constant vigil on the fugitive's 3M's is the key to success. Money, Mama and the Main squeeze are the 3M's. The fugitives that get caught are always done in by their inability to cut ties with at least one of the 3M's.

Finally, six months in, Céline went on her yearly sabbatical to visit her mom in Montreal. This was in keeping with what she had done every year since she had been working in L.A. She always flew in, stayed a full seven days, and then flew back out on a Sunday. I managed to surprise her late one night by hiding in her bedroom. We could only risk that one connection and soon, I was back in Holland, once again sad and depressed. I started to daydream about giving the money back, starting over and going back to law school. I could see myself waking up with Céline every morning. We would have our coffee in the kitchen while we talked about our plans for the day. It was crazy. The people we had burned were not the type to forgive and forget, even if I could come up with a way to return the $1.4 million I had already spent. Seeing her again, touching her, making love, it was all too much. I missed her more than ever. I had to find a way.

The big Arrowhead water truck pulled up to the curb at 1805

Beverly Drive, Beverly Hills, California. The old-style house was well kept. The front door was fifteen feet inside a front gate that was just four feet from the curb. The home had been a gift from one of Céline's more grateful clients. I swung down out of the truck's cab, glanced in both directions, and hoisted a 5-gallon bottle of Arrowhead's finest onto my right shoulder. It is amazing what you can get for ten grand on short notice in L.A. I got the fully stocked truck and everything right down to my starched uniform shirt with the name Bud stitched above the pocket.

Nobody seemed to be on the sidewalk on this sunny, perfect L.A. day. I cleared the walk and closed the gate behind me. I was in. I looked up, surprised to see Céline standing in the doorway with just the glass door separating us. She wore her morning robe, the purple one I loved so much. She must have sensed I was coming back this morning because I had not been able to tell her. It would've been too risky. She didn't realize it was me at first, then our eyes met and her recognition was like the sunrise. I wanted to run to her and wrap myself around her but I didn't dare take the chance. I had to stay in character. I allowed myself a smile and the sparks jumped between us. Slowly I continued walking. I'm Bud, just delivering a customer's water. Remember... Bud. Céline's lips parted, her tongue moistening her upper, then her lower, tantalizing lip.

A hot burning poker suddenly tore through my upturned right arm. The water bottle I carried crashed to the walkway, the cold, wet liquid splashing onto my feet. To my right, I saw a middle aged Italian man in a very nice suit and tie walking toward me. He was overdressed for the occasion and smiling like a game show host.

"Good to finally see you, Nick," the man said. My eyes zoomed in to focus on his index finger wrapped tightly around the trigger of the gun in his hand. Céline screamed. I was still walking toward her but I seemed to be losing ground. She pushed open the glass door and ran toward me. An explosion tore into my mid section and ripped open my belly. I looked down to see blood rushing from my stomach. The ground rushed up and caught me. I could see Céline, like an angel now dressed in white; she seemed to be floating above me. Darkness, deep, deep darkness enveloped me as I heard another shot ring out. Suddenly a bright light appeared and I could see an angel standing at the entrance to a tunnel beckoning me onward. His lips did not move, but I could sense what he was saying.

"You will forever be with your love now, watching out for her, guiding her.

Jesus' Loneliest Daughter

I had been in Portland for only about a week when I got sick. It was winter and not all that cold out. I had been hiding in L. A. for so long though, that the Northwestern weather felt arctic to my tanned skin and bones. I was staying at the General Inn on the second floor. The General was just as you might picture it. Barely hanging on, waiting on urban renewal to put a wrecking ball bullet through its decaying lobby of a brain. I didn't know a single soul in Portland. That was the whole reason I had fled there. The guy who sold me a quarter ounce of pot seemed friendly enough, but people always do when you're handing them money.

Gina was a hooker. A fact I had a hard time understanding. She was much too young and pretty for that job. She had a certain softness about her that hookers do not possess. I had not paid to take the ride myself, but her room was next door to mine. The paper-thin walls were no help as I lay in the dark trying to shut out the sound of other guys getting their forty dollars-worth of Gina. I had nodded to her a couple of times on the stairs but we had not spoken. She was only nineteen years old, I would soon find out. She could have easily been one of the beautiful super models I had been paid to photograph back in L.A.

Just one more reason I thought I was hallucinating from fever -- I awoke to find her wiping my forehead with a wet cloth. "Your fever's breakin'. I gave you four Tylenol." Not knowing what to say, I just stared at the small mole on her cheek. She asked sweetly, "Feelin' better?"

"I think so," I mumbled between terrible bouts of a hacking cough. Each time I wheezed it felt like I was breaking off another piece of my broken lung. "I'm goin' out to get us some breakfast. Want anything else?" She was standing over me now, wearing a loose blouse and short shorts. I felt my Johnson come to life as I realized how big and brown her eyes were. After all, I was sick, not dead.

"No, that's fine," I lied, as she walked to the door.

We feasted on waffles and scrambled eggs, neither of us talking. She spoke first, "You haven't eaten in three days." She smiled at me like a nurse. I ran my hand through my greasy hair.

"God, I don't remember the last time I had a shower."

"You were out of your head. I had my friend Ricky come over and give you a shot of antibiotics." She must have seen the horrified look on my face. "It's alright, Ricky's in med school. An intern actually." I checked my arms for needle marks. They were clean. "Oh he don't miss. He's a junkie too. He's plannin' to quit, soon as he gets his practice set up." I was shocked again.

"When did you? I mean, how did you?"

She laughed. I suddenly realized she had the most perfect teeth I had ever seen.

"Every morning you would get up and go to breakfast. That day, I didn't even hear you moving around over here except for the coughing," she said. "That night I heard you tossing and screaming, so I came over to check on you."

"Really? What was I saying?"

"Crazy stuff about the ocean and dolphins and you kept calling out for a Michelle, I think it was." I didn't respond. She pulled a bottle of red cough syrup out of a white paper bag, uncorked it and took a powerful swig.

"This is for you. It's loaded with codeine. Believe me, it helps," she laughed. I took my turn with the bottle, and then I looked at the label. Immediately I started to cough. I ran to the sink and coughed up what seemed like a bucket of green, slimy mucus.

"Told ya. Ricky says there's a terrible bug goin' round. Turns into pneumonia. He says it's killin' two or three people a day at County General. That's where he works."

I never asked how she got into my room or why she had bothered to come to the aid of a total stranger. Gina was nice enough not to ask me about Michelle. She sat on the bed with one leg curled up under her talking and laughing. We talked for hours, mostly about how magical the world was when we were kids. We survived on cough syrup, and sweet and sour soup from Dragon Palace across the street. She had complete faith in the healing powers of those two remedies. And she was right. By the next day, I was on my feet again and starting to feel human. We had some time on our hands anyway because Gina stopped seeing clients and I didn't have a job yet. For the next five days she gave me the newbie's tour of Portland.

She loved the rose garden, especially in winter. We shared a joint there as dusk fell on the snow-covered city below, waking up the streetlights. We laughed at all the drones rushing home from their life-crushing jobs. She showed me the hidden path that snaked from downtown to the Willamette River. There was one trail that led right up to a new subdivision of Mc-mansions. Gina thought it hilarious that the houses had been built on top of what had once been an old garbage dump. On Saturday, we walked among the booths at the City Market. I bought her an angel made of silver, with wings that lit up when you touched it. I pinned it on her lapel. She really was my angel. I would have died in that cheap hotel room had she not come to my rescue.

I dreamed of saving Gina from the terrible life she had chosen for herself. I knew that what she did for money was joined with her burning love for the one thing in life that had never let her down. Heroin. Sweet, sweet H. China-white when she was lucky. Mexican brown when she wasn't. I knew this because I wasn't a complete stranger to the lure of H. Jones myself.

I had been only seventeen when I found out my first love, Sheila, my childhood sweetheart, was gone forever. I ran into the arms of Morpheus and, after my trip down, told myself that it would do just fine as a replacement for her love. I started out with a sniff here and a sniff there until that just didn't get it anymore. I bugged my junkie friend, Joe, for days until he finally gave in and bought me my first ticket on the main line. Soon I was able to hit the vein myself. I was hooked. A full-blown junkie. I went on an eight-month run that damn near ended without my eighteenth birthday arriving. Luckily, I was in the South where the supply doesn't always match the desire. We couldn't cop anywhere. I was aching and so puke sick for two weeks that I swore I would never touch the stuff again. Of course, as soon as I could score again I was off on another run. The next time we ran out I swore off it completely. I kicked cold turkey, spending most of the next two weeks lying in a hot bath trying to ease the pain. I had finally unlocked the secret that you never can see while wrapped in the comforting arms of the junk man. The only time you're truly happy is after that first shot. Every time after that, you're just chasing the dream, trying to catch that elusive feeling again. You never do.

I knew Gina needed to get out of Portland to have a chance. "Gina, I know people in modeling agencies in L.A. Believe me, if I send them shots of you, you'll be in demand. Five hundred dollars a day would be easy for you." She laughed and shook her head.

"I hate L.A. It's always sunny there. I'll keep Portland. At least you can count on the rain." I guess it's a testament to how much alike we were that I understood exactly what she meant.

We laughed and talked some more. She had been abused by a Step Dad and her mother had only one emotion for her too-pretty daughter -- jealousy. Those things were bad enough, but I suspected there was something else. Something so terrible that had bruised her heart as a child that she could not bring herself to speak of it.

Gina was a great listener and she soon knew everything about me. Everything except how I had killed Michelle's love for me; killed it so dead that she could never get it back. Wounded as we both were Gina and I clung to each other like two kids lost at the fair. I talked her into moving with me to a much nicer hotel where we had our own kitchen. Gina stopped 'dating' as she called it and encouraged by me she joined AA and got off the needle. I devoted myself to helping her kick completely. I started her on a vitamin, mineral program to help build her health back up. I massaged her aching muscles and made her soothing hot teas of all kinds. I kept refilling a hot bathtub full of water for her to soak in and when she got her appetite back I made sure she had the most nutritious foods to eat. After three weeks she started to feel better and soon she was making plans to go back to school and learn a profession so she could make it in the world. Gina and I were celebrating her forty-five days clean. I was cooking her favorite pasta dish when I realized we needed more sauce. She jumped up, grabbed the keys and ran to the supermarket. After searching for her for three days I found my car parked out front with a note stuck to the steering wheel. "I can't do this, I'm sorry" the note read.

Gina didn't have a pimp. She was very proud of that fact. "I own my own business," she liked to say. Gina had a very commercial approach to her job. Money was always paid up front. Protection, as in safe sex, was mandatory. She didn't do drugs that johns brought her. She told me once that she wasn't there to party, just to deliver a service and collect her pay. It was all that simple to her. She made one more attempt at getting clean with my help but she didn't last nearly as long as she had the first time.

I was the one the police called when they found her. I had gotten a job in the up and coming world of TV advertising there in Portland. I had rejoined the straight work-a-day drones. Three months had passed and I was living in a trendy apartment on the North side. I had given Gina a key in case she was ever in trouble or needed out of the elements. She had used it only once. I woke up one Sunday morning with a bad hangover and found her wrapped in my arms. It was the only time I had ever seen her cry. I held her for an hour or so until she felt better. I wasn't sure what had happened to her. I only know it must have been terrible to shake her because she was the toughest person I had ever known. We talked of going to breakfast but when I got out of the shower she was gone.

The cops said they found my expired California driver's license and my new business card on her dresser. She loved my pic on that old license. She said I looked just like Starsky or Hutch, she couldn't remember which. Gina died alone, a needle in her arm. I paid for a small service and her burial. It wasn't enough, but it was all I had left to offer her. She had saved my life. I could not save hers. I can still close my eyes and see her perfect smile. The cops had found her mom's Nebraska phone number in her effects. They called to inform her of her daughter's death but, as soon as they got Gina's name out, she cussed at them and hung up. She never even found out why they were calling.

It was just the preacher and I at the service. I would have gladly paid him another hundred dollars to say what he chose to say on his own. He spoke as if he knew Gina. "Jesus walked among the ladies of the night. He believed all were his daughters. All deserving of his grace. All saved in his name. Perhaps Gina was Jesus' loneliest daughter. We know that doesn't matter now because Gina is at peace. She is in a much better place, far removed from those that would hurt her. Gina has been saved from the trials of this earthly world."

I squeezed the silver angel in my hand as hard as I could, as I tried to remember her touch. I looked down and saw that the stick pin had dug into my flesh and blood had run down my arm. I stepped out of the church into another perfect Portland day. It had started to rain. Gina would have loved that.

Once Upon A Time In Vegas

Rick didn't mind taking shit. He was known for flipping plenty of it himself but, about the Irish thing, and from a fuckin' new guy? Not gonna happen. The kid had been out from Kansas City for all of two weeks and he had already found fourteen different ways he thought things could be run better. Slapping him into his place was more than justified. The fact that Gloria had ragged Rick all morning over some little nothin' over nothin' about nothin' meant Rick packed the full force of his body into the right he launched into the kid. There was a loud "SNAP - CLOSE ON," – Rick's knuckles smashing skin into teeth and bone. The kid's knees didn't buckle so much as they just folded up under him. He dropped straight into his footprint, like a controlled casino demolition. Rick's fist recoil was so quick it was like it hadn't really happened.

Rocco laughed so hard he started to snort. Finally, he downed his Scotch-rocks and regained the power of speech. "I can only hope you didn't fuck up his smile, he's emceeing the lounge tomorrow night." The lounge featured showgirls and comics but somebody had to be there to hold it all together, to fill in time between the gigs. Rocco among other things ran "VIP," the big spenders, and he had a hundred ways to make sure the whales kept playing long after they should have been on the plane home to the little woman. But, lately Rocco seemed to always be in the lounge. "Boy got a mouth on him, but hell, that's why he's a good emcee," Rick nodded.

"He don't wake up no smarter than he fuckin' was, his funeral's gonna need an emcee."

Rick had been running things in the desert for the outfit for as long as anyone remembered. He first came to Vegas in the sixties straight from Mr. C's produce business in Kansas City. Vegas was a six month a year gig then, strictly a summer attraction. Now it was 1972 and Vegas had become a lot more than that. Just one of the many big changes blowing through the desert. Vegas was Rick's from the day he stepped off the plane. Pardon me, Frank, but you want the city that never sleeps, it's Las Vegas, baby. Inside these cool cocoons of majesty, the lighting never changes and the drinks never stop flowing. No clocks around to distract a player with mundane remembrances of schedules and responsibilities. No night! No day! This place was made for Rick and, like the town, he didn't sleep. He might grab a quick forty winks here or there, be gone for two hours tops. That meant none of the underlings had time to steal from the cash skim headed east. Mr. C loved the fuck out of that.

Rick didn't just oversee the Fremont although it was the first property he had gone to work on and both his main office and the suite he lived in were on the top floor. Mr. C, or the old man, as the other guys called him was most proud of what Rick had managed to do with the casino and the hotel there. Anyone who was anyone, knew Rick was the man at the Fremont but, what most players didn't know, was that he was also the man at the Hacienda, the Landmark and, most importantly, the Stardust.

Rick's being Irish didn't even bother the oldest members of the crew. Sure the inside guys liked to bust on him, call him a potato-eater sometimes. But let someone from another family even mention it and they had better be ready to fight. Everyone in the outfit knew Rick's history and what Rick's dad, William Riley had meant to the old man. It was the winter of '57 in Apalachin, New York. The bosses from all the families nationwide were at Joseph, "Joe the Barber," Barbara's estate to do one thing, divide up the United States. Rick's dad, Riley to the crew, was Mr. C's driver and bodyguard. When the Feds broke through the Gambino guys guarding the gate, one of the gate guards managed to radio a warning to the kitchen. While the other "made" men were running through the snowy woods tossing guns and cash aside, Riley, an expert horseman, had ushered Mr. C to the barn. He had spotted the two mares when he scouted the property earlier. The two things Riley brought home from the Korean War were a skill with horses and a sixth sense when something wasn't right. While the Feds were rounding up all the other freezing mob bosses from the woods, Riley was placing the old man safely into a taxi out on the county road. The value of that save could not be stated in dollars. Not being publicly identified as a mobster along with the sixty or so that were rounded up, left Mr. C with the power of anonymity. He had not failed to capitalize on it. Rick's dad died of a heart attack a year later, the week Rick turned sixteen. The old man vowed that very day that Riley's son would do well. Straight working stiffs could never understand the loyalty reserved for guys in the outfit. The deepest level of that loyalty along with the history they shared is what Mr. C had with Rick. The son his wife had never been able to give him is the way Mr. C looked at it. There was a bigger reason Mr. C's man in Vegas had to be as solid as a son. The Nevada Black Book had been created in 1960 to keep those with 'notorious and unsavory reputations' out of the Las Vegas gambling business. Mr. C along with his older brother Carl had been the first two entrants. The selections were arbitrary but were aimed at organized crime. This meant Mr. C could not set foot in a casino without heavy fines and threat of arrest.

The spot most folks had reserved in their hearts for God and country was the exact position Rick placed Mr. C and Gloria. Gloria was only ten years younger than Rick, but she looked a full ten years younger than her age. That, coupled with the fact that Gloria was a full on ten, made folks wonder what Gloria's attraction was to Rick. It probably helped his chances that there was more than one reason he was known as Rick the Rod, but it was the overwhelming scent of power that really kept Gloria turned on. Their eyes met as Rick powered across the card room. His light gray suit and blood red tie caught Gloria's eye against the backdrop of Bermuda shorts and loud plaid tops. Rick was there to eye up a dealer who had been sloppy on too many occasions. Gloria had been running back and forth to the card room all night. She was trying to interest her new husband in laying down his winning hand so he could come upstairs to seal this marriage deal. It was already the second full night of their honeymoon and he had yet to seal their union. A fact that was making Gloria more and more anxious with each trip up and down the elevator. Rick just remembered the look. Their eyes met and a shiver swept over him, freezing his brain like a visit to Tasty Freeze. The only feeling in his entire body was a stirring in his trousers. Five minutes later, she was on her knees in the kitchen pantry knobbing the object of her affection. After which of course she informed Rick that she was not really that type of gal. Twenty-four hours later, the First National Bank of Ohio opened with her ex-husband seated very stiffly behind his desk, Vice President Placard askew. All her hubby knew for sure was that a man would be there at 4:30 that afternoon with legal papers annulling his new marriage to Gloria and he would be signing them.

Rick and Gloria were now an item. It was love. A fact Rocco would've wagered the whole house against. "Rick was a guy didn't love his own damn mother." But they lasted. Rick was different after he met Gloria, on that everyone agreed. The exact reasons why would take a little longer to understand.

If the Strip was Disneyland as a whorehouse then the Stardust was the strip on Adderall. Everything great about Vegas, but more focused. The Stardust was one of the original casinos and, after it was remodeled in '64, it was the hip happening place to be on the strip. When you rolled up that driveway with a million neon bulbs twinkling, no question, you had arrived. Even the sign out front with purple and pink planets blasting light sixty miles into the night-time sky confirmed that you were out of this world. Lefty "Rose" Rosenthal was the Stardust to most folks. He opened the first sports booking room in Vegas at the Stardust. He was well known and flashy and that too was good for business. What most folks didn't know was that Rose was run by Mr. C, which meant he too reported to Rick.

The more Rick could remain in the background the better. Rick modeled himself after the old man and the major lesson not lost on Rick was the fact that Mr. C was the king of the world, at least partly, because he was unknown. The people outside the outfit had no idea who he was and even the guys on the inside had no idea how much he controlled.

For all the great things the Stardust had going for it, the thing Rick loved the most, was the roof. The East Tower, as it was known, was added on during the remodel, at the same time as the Olympic-sized pool below. Only nine stories tall, it offered up a commanding and breathtaking view of the Vegas strip. You took dames up there, they loved the view. Gloria loved to go up there and get it on. In fact, Gloria loved to get it on anywhere publicly where they might get caught.

Still, that was not primarily what Rick liked about it. Mob movies loved to show some poor loser getting his knees busted. Thing was, that wasn't always practical. The other movie thing that drove Rick crazy was when the Boss sent his goons to kill some poor sap that owed him money. As Rick liked to ask Rocco, "How fuckin' smart is that?"

Thing was, you catch some guys "spooking" at the blackjack table, maybe even find a dealer in on it. One little trip to the roof could get their mind right. You put Tuffy or Carl the Plumber, onto one end of a rope, the other end tied securely around the punk's ankles. You swing the thief while he takes an upside-down view of the strip, nine stories below. Believe me, if any other guys are in on it you are gonna know right away who they are and where to find em'. Better still, the only mark you leave is the one imprinted permanently on their brain. Thirty minutes later, your dealer is back at work with no visible damage, except for maybe the load in his pants. Here's the payoff to the whole gag. Say one of em' gets loose, breaks free and ends up eating the concrete below. Not a problem. Just one more gambling suicide. The Vegas P.D. loves an easy wrap-up like that. The last time that happened, they had a suicide death cert by the next day. So, you got no worries about someone finding a body. There was always a room on the ninth floor on that side of the hotel left open and the front desk was ready to dummy the registration. A more complete deal had never been invented.

Rocco was a guy could never leave well enough alone, though. He got Belinder, the hotel carpenter, to construct a narrow deck with a handrail just big enough for two people hanging off the lip of the building. It was a lover's perch if ever there was one. You had the feeling, standing on it, that you were suspended in space. In the floor were two imperceptible trap doors, each independent of the other. In fact, when one was open the other had to be closed. The setup was such, a person could be standing at the rail and, suddenly, the way back to the roof became just open air. Of course, if the right button was pushed and that door was closed, the trap door at the rail would fly open.

Belinder had installed the controls in a hidden recess in the concrete post next to the heating and cooling system a good twenty-five feet from the deck itself. Rocco took Rick up to look at it. "You gotta love this. Fuckers are walking the plank." Rick walked up to it, warily testing the handrail. "Take the whole thing out, fuckin' thing bothers me." Rick didn't like change. Why fix it if ain't broke kinda thing, but like most changes Rocco snuck in, after awhile Rick got used to it. His only order that stuck was two keys only. Maintenance, security, even Rose himself did not get a key. Access to the roof by anyone meant Rick or Rocco had let them up there.

Rick finally got comfortable with the new deck after he saw how much Gloria got turned on making love on it. Gloria wasn't just a play thing for Rick though; she had helped Rick solve a serious financial problem. That was the cash cow turned cash vacuum known as the Office Park. Like so many things, it only makes sense if you start at the beginning. Rick had gotten into the porn business by accident really. They called it the Office Park because the operation was located in a low key office/warehouse park just like a hundred other mixed-use parks springing up all over Vegas. You walked in to a receptionist cubicle with the alias company name in bold letters over her desk. If you were expected, she buzzed you into the warehouse area. There were three other offices in the hallway. The rest of the space had been converted to home interiors. Three separate bedroom sets, a kitchen, a living room, a study, a good-size pool and Jacuzzi with a skylight over it.

There was even a storage area full of plants and various styles of furniture. Set designers could approximate five different interior house styles, all of them "Early Valley." Oh yeah, the beginning.

Lumpy was a five-foot-two, 225-lb. lesbian who had taken money her parents gave her for college and sunk every penny of it into making porn. And, crazy enough, from day one it made money. Lumpy knew the market and, unlike so many other failures, she knew distribution. She negotiated a strong deal with the largest distributor on the west coast and her films sold worldwide. The problem for Lumpy was the same one that had brought down many a much more famous director. She fell in love with her main star. For a while, the romance actually worked. When Sindy Love switched teams once again, back to men, Lumpy was heartbroken. This heartbreak caused her to do copious amounts of Peruvian marching powder, eat Fudgesicles, and gamble. Somehow, over that first love lost weekend, the pit boss at the Fremont let Lumpy get into the house for $300 large. "This dame is loaded," he told Rick. "I'll have the cash in-house by close of business today."

Problem was when Tuffy and Carl the Plumber busted into Lumpy's office; the fancy pink safe was empty. Lumpy had stopped making new product four months ago when the love affair started and now she was too depressed. Tuffy got on the office phone to Rick and informed him that the primary inventory of their new business consisted of slightly-used furniture with jism stains. At first, Rick thought the way to salvation was to put Lumpy back into business. With all the cash going directly back to the house of course. She had been a success, after all. Problem was that was the old, more confident Lumpy. Enter Randy California.

Randy California was a forty-something, blonde surfer type. His nickname did double duty. He grew up in Redondo Beach and, of course, he looked like a Californian. Like many a West Coast refugee, he came to Vegas to run away from his past. Randy had gone to high school with Robert Bonner, who went on to become the most sought-after action director in Hollywood. Bonner had helped his old high school pal into the business by giving him associate producer credit on a film that went on to gross mega millions. Suddenly, Randy California was in demand as a producer, even though he had been just a gofer on his buddy's movie. He went on to a short but successful career as a producer. In just a six year span he earned a producer's credit on two more very successful films.

Unfortunately Randy's slide to the bottom came just as quickly as his meteoric rise to the top. He developed a terrible drinking problem, probably because he felt like a fraud. Although there are plenty of producers who are drunks, they are quiet drunks. Randy developed a bad habit he liked to repeat while on a bender, usually about an hour before he completely passed out. He would go through the closely guarded, private, studio directory calling and threatening the biggest Hollywood stars. The studios employ guys that handle things like that and they soon showed up, beating Randy so badly that he would never regain full use of his brain. He drifted out to Las Vegas and ended up as a greeter at the Fremont.

Rick reasoned that if Randy could produce Hollywood films, he could easily throw together some cheap pornos, even if he was now using fewer brain cells. So, Randy was reborn and soon had steady product rolling out of the Office Park. At the end of the first year, Rick had been able to retire Lumpy's debt to the casino which was $350,000 with vig. Two months into the second year, Randy California had a massive brain aneurysm. His body seized and jerked forward, falling onto the two lovers he had been directing. Randy California died right in the middle of the big money shot.

When Rick met Gloria, the Office Park had been dark for three months while Rick considered his options. Soon as Gloria found out about it, she threw herself into rescuing the business. Gloria grew up in a family of bankers and she had always been anxious to prove that she was just as capable as any of her brothers in turning a profit. Gloria treated the Office Park like it was any, for profit operation.

From the minute Gloria took over, the Office Park became a moneymaker. Rick, ever faithful to the old man, added Mr. C's cut to the skim suitcases that were forever winging their way east to Kansas City. By the end of Gloria's first year running things, the size of the old man's share had become huge. Mr. C knew the money was from Rick's side business, but Rick made sure he didn't know what that side business was. Mr. C was funny that way, he was strictly old school, and Rick was sure he wouldn't approve. Gloria ran a tight ship. She hired no-nonsense directors and cameramen. She got rid of the tough, biker chicks that had populated Lumpy's films. She hired male and female actors who would fit right in at an upper-class social event. This gave the films more of a classy look and feel. Something the porn industry had been dying for, evidently.

Before Gloria, the crews that made these films were usually men and women on their way down, Hollywood types who for one reason or another could no longer work in legitimate film. Gloria reversed that trend. She hired young talents that were ambitious and on their way up. Their success with Gloria propelled some of them into big-time jobs on studio feature films. The last time Rick and Gloria had visited L.A. they were treated to dinner at Le Dome by one of Gloria's former directors who was filming a tent pole for Disney. The kid got on Rick's last nerve when he spent the whole dinner complimenting Gloria. He kept saying that Gloria could easily be a big time producer in Hollywood. "Hell, you could cut the budget in half and deliver twice the film this USC kid is putting together." Of course, Gloria ate it up with a spoon. On the other hand, Rick already had serious problems with Hollywood and was ready to discourage her before the kid even took a second breath.

Earlier that year some Hollywood pussy had come up with "The Godfather." Rick would never forgive him. It caused the family a lot of grief and aggravation. Now, in addition to posers, you had real outfit guys dressed in three-piece suits and wide-brim hats. It was hard to hold a serious meet with a crew that looked like they were about to bust out into song and dance. Maybe do the opening number from "Guys and Dolls." The Hollywood treatment didn't do dick for Rick, but Gloria was in heaven. Front row seats at the Hollywood Bowl. Stuffing a rented Rolls-Royce with glitzy shopping bags on Rodeo Drive. Rick was, of course, chained to Las Vegas and soon Gloria was visiting L.A. without him, going about once a month and staying longer each time. Her extended stays had become the main subject of their fights. Rick couldn't accuse her of neglecting the Office Park, hell; the business was cranking out over a million dollars a year. He sure as hell could complain though, about her not being there for him as his old lady. She eventually agreed to limit her trips and spend more time seeing to his needs. Yet, sly as a fox, she attended to his needs but dreamed about making the jump to legitimate film and moving to L.A. without Rick.

When Split Finger Phil showed up from Chicago, it didn't come as a complete surprise. Rick had heard from Mr. C that Chicago was unhappy with their cut. The new Chicago boss apparently thought he could get another 5% by whining and throwing his weight around. When Rick saw Split Finger Phil dressed in a pin-striped suit, vest, and spats he took it as a sign. Phil was a made man, been around for ages. Here he was dressed like some Hollywood pussy straight out of that mob movie Rick hated. This to Rick meant one thing. Chicago was about to make a move on the Kansas City outfit.

Virtually everyone, including the Feds, thought when it came to Vegas, Chicago was in charge. That impression was more than fine with Mr. C but in reality the old man himself had complete control of the Teamsters Pension Fund. Chicago's power had dwindled with the disappearance of Jimmy Hoffa. The Teamster's Pension Fund loaned the money to build the damn casinos, after all. The pension fund was run by Teamsters President Roy Wilson and Mr. C ran Roy Wilson. The skim went directly to Kansas City and, out of that; Mr. C gave Chicago their cut.

As instructed by the old man, Rick gave Phil the complete tour of the operation top to bottom. Not the Office Park, that of course was all Rick's. He showed him downtown, the strip, how the eye in the sky worked, even had Rose take him along to the taping of his TV show. They let him win a few hands of poker, and then Rose sent up two of the town's sweetest working girls and had them stay the whole night. So, Phil was feeling well fucked and relaxed as Tuffy drove Rick and his guest to the airport. As they passed an empty patch of desert, Rick leaned forward from the back seat, planted his .38 at the base of Split Finger Phil's skull and put one right into his brain stem. Tuffy dropped Rick at his car at the airport. Carl the Plumber got in and they gave Split Finger Phil his one-way ride to the desert. That dealt with, Rick could get back to running the day-to-day. The old man would have to fade the heat, no doubt. To kill a made member without a sit down, you just didn't do it. That's why Rick hadn't asked Tuffy or Carl to do the deed. No way they had the juice to get away with it themselves. Rick was sure though that the old man would approve, given the attempted takeover and what was at stake. Time proved his guess had been right and Chicago got the message. Things were gonna stay the same.

Rick was feeling good. Here he was with Gloria, a month after planting one right on the kid's kisser. Now he sat laughing at the kid's jokes and clapping for him. Gloria and her best friend Linda had dragged him into the lounge to see the kid's act. Jerry Martin was the stage name Rocco had given him and the tourists couldn't get enough. Linda, according to Gloria, was crazy about him. He was a tall, good looking kid, Rick had to admit and, like Rocco had said, the kid did have a deep radio voice. One bigger plus for

Linda was that Jerry was also a workout nut. Gloria went with Linda at least four times a week to the gym. That's where Linda had met Jerry and, according to Gloria, it was love at first sight. Of course, Linda had said that about her last three boyfriends, as Rick recalled. Since Gloria and Rick always doubled with Linda and whoever the current "Mr. Right" was, Rick would need to get used to hanging out with the kid. Jerry Martin wasn't just filling time now, he was doing his own jokes and singing his own songs and the crowd loved it. Hell, Rick felt he could make nice, and be a sport, but there was one thing still bothering him about the kid. In Rick's experience, whenever he had taken someone down with physical force, and he had plenty of experience with it, one of two things happened when dealing with them afterward. Either they cowered a bit and were overly nice to protect themselves from another beating. Or they were nice but seemed to hold something in reserve, some hope, however remote, that they would get a chance to retaliate. He could always see which camp they fell into by the way they looked at him. With this kid, Jerry, or whatever his name really was, he could sense neither. In the few times their paths had crossed it was like the kid was a blank slate, like the beat down had never happened and that bugged the hell out of

Rick. He sat daydreaming about taking the kid over to the roof of the Stardust and putting him on Rocco's plank for a short walk, when Gloria's voice brought him back to reality. "Linda wants us to join her and Jerry for drinks after the show."

Surprisingly enough, Rick was enjoying himself more than he had in a long while. Gloria had been treating him like she used to treat him when they had first met. They had started out, the four of them in the bar over at Circus Circus. It turns out the kid's favorite drink was a White Russian, same as his. They set out to match each other Russian for Russian. Kid could hold his liquor too. Crazy thing was the kid grew up on the Kansas side just like Rick had. He had gone to the same high school as Rick, years later of course, and the kid had actually memorized Rick's golden gloves' boxing stats. The more they talked, the more they drank, the more Rick really started to like the kid. By the time they moved on to the Hacienda and vodka shots, Rick and Jerry were laughing at each other's bad jokes in their own corner, while the girls sat a few feet away gossiping about which actress was getting it by what actor and how her husband was taking it. They loved that kind of stuff. Linda had a condo just a block off the strip. Finally they went there for a nightcap. Turns out Linda had a pool table, and Jerry and

Rick played back-to-back games of Rotation. Rick was entertaining Jerry and the girls with his drunken shooting and his deep knowledge of the history of pool. "Rotation's tha' thing...it, it, what was I, oh yeah, Minnesota Fats ran the table nine times in a game of Rotation...eight ball, it's shit...any, any, what tha' hell was I sayin'?" They were all cracking up at Rick's condition since no one, including Gloria, had ever seen him that drunk. Rick was always in charge, always "on duty," Gloria liked to tell her friends. Rick didn't remember ever feeling that great, so when Gloria fished the Stardust roof keys out of his pocket as he was driving home he just steered the car into the Stardust parking lot. Hell yeah, they would get it on as the sun came up over the desert. What could be better?

If Gloria needed that level of danger to get off...Rick was ready. He'd be just as happy being a dedicated missionary in the bed at home, but he wasn't about to let Gloria down. One little toenail of sun was starting to peek out over the floor of the desert. Still it was mushy dark out. Gloria had Rick all hot and excited. Rick was leaning on the handrail of Rocco's wooden deck and Gloria's mouth had worked her way down Rick's chest, before she dropped to her knees. Unzipping his pants, she leaned back a bit and Rick could swear he heard a whistle. At the same instant Gloria rolled backward, Rick heard the hinge below him – CATCH - SNAP OPEN. Strange thing was, it was Gloria who took the ride straight down. INSTANTLY SOBER, Rick yelled. "Noooo," as he stared down at what had been his beautiful Gloria, in a heap on the walkway. Rick's hand darted inside his jacket for his .38 and found an EMPTY HOLSTER. The roof was all aglow in those warm sunrise tones. Rick blinked twice but the image didn't clear. It definitely was the kid standing at the heating/AC with his hand on the deck control button. Rick dived for the roof just as the floor below him disappeared. Rick rolled to break his fall and came up holding his back-up piece, his .22 pistol. Jerry Martin bobbed left and then right before scrambling toward the stairway through tears of his own. "I'm sorry Gloria." he kept mumbling.

The scam started to clear in Rick's mind. Gloria had made a deal with the kid. Maybe she was doin' him, maybe she wasn't. Rick didn't care to find out. Either way, the plan had been to drop Rick. Really drop Rick. When the moment of truth came, the kid pulled the wrong switch, that's all. Rick caught up with him just before he was able to get the stairwell door open. Jerry fought back but Rick was in a rage that four able-bodied men could not have controlled. Rick kicked the door shut just as Jerry spun around with a lie on his lips. Rick slammed his pistol into the kid's face. Rick whipped him with the gun twice more before pressing the barrel into his temple. His trigger finger shaking and trembling, he pressed his face up against Jerry's mug.

"No, that's too good for you. Too easy," Rick said as he tossed the gun aside. Jerry squinted at him through a stream of blood running into his eyes and tried to speak.

"I didn, didn mea..." Rick cut him off with a hard slap to the lips.

"Don't you say her name." Rick yelled.

Tears were streaming down Rick's face as he drug Jerry across the roof by his jacket while he continued pummeling him in the face. When they reached the edge, Rick lifted Jerry up and swung him like he was an empty suit. Jerry's jacket caught air for a second, and then he was gone. The kid didn't make a sound as he hurtled downward, just a loud SCHLAPP as he landed.

The next night, Rich Little filled in as emcee as he was headlining down the street at the Sands and owed Rocco a favor. As the voices of Sinatra and the entire Rat pack filled the lounge Rick assured Rocco they'd find a replacement that was better than the kid had ever been. Rocco laughed and snorted the way he always had, yet Rocco remained quiet as a tombstone when Rick told him he'd soon find another Gloria. They both knew that was a lie.

The Indian Cowboy

I hung a hard right turn allowing just enough time for the rear end of the Lincoln to straighten out, and then I gunned it. The big Lincoln V-8 ate up the pavement and in no time at all we were clocking 105. The Lincoln had never been my car of choice but a strange thing happens when you live long enough to see your forties. Your favorite relatives start dying *en masse*. The latest to step on a Rainbow was my Uncle Roscoe. This silver 2006 Lincoln Town car had been his parting gift. Uncle Roscoe had not used his precious remaining time to tell me what I soon found out. The Lincoln was one helluva road car. Fast, responsive and smooth. It cruised better at a hundred than at seventy. I was just the man to give the Lincoln its freedom. Why not? We had nothing but straight and true interstate through the Nevada desert and my $1,200 illegal radar detector was pinging back to me. No, singing really. All clear...all clear.

I spent most of my twenties studying medicinal uses of native plants among American Indian tribes. This is where the first part of my nickname came from. The second half refers to how I do things. At least that's what Doc tells me and he's the one who stuck me with it all those years ago. Doc's nickname deserves a longer explanation. One we will get to in due time. The Indian Cowboy, yours truly, and my trusty Watson, Doctor Construction, were on a mission. As I drove, Doc was catching up on much needed sleep in the passenger seat. We were once again out to solve a crime..... No, no, that's not what the two of us really do. What we do is UN-solve crimes. Since the passage of the Patriot Act and God knows how many other draconian laws and regulations, more and more good Americans are finding themselves locked up for no damn good reason. Getting justice for those wronged folks, that's what the good Doctor and I are all about. We usually get involved only after all other means are exhausted and then only at the request of a family member of the wrongly convicted party. We are lucky to have top-notch attorneys who assist us at every turn. Attorneys who still believe in the rule of law, American justice and that wacky thing called the Constitution.

Doctor Construction opened his eyes and yawned. "Want me to drive awhile?"

"Yeah," I told him, "In about 2,000 miles. That robin's-egg-speckled pharmaceutical speed is just coming on." Doc stared at me a minute.

"I thought you swore off all illicit substances other than your sacred herb?"

"True," I said. "Trucker gave me one helluva deal though. Besides, it's mission-dependent. Okay?"

"How long have I been asleep?"

I forced my wired lips into a smile. "You crashed hard my brethren, somewhere around Tupelo... and we are about to cross out of Nevada into the freedom state of California."

"My God, I've been out for days," Doc said, a look of mock terror on his face.

"Tupelo, New Mexico, I think it was."

Doc didn't respond. He just rolled his left eyebrow at me while he reached into the cooler and pulled out two Red Bulls and his jumbo coffee mug. He poured the Bulls into his mug like a pro bartender. Reaching into one of the many hidden compartments, Doc retrieved a nearly full bottle of Jack and carefully poured just the right amount into the mix. I eyed him suspiciously.

"Breakfast?"

"Mission-dependent," he said.

"Good, once you're awake, how about reaching into the back

seat and popping open that file?" Which file?" he asked.

"The one that reminds us what kind of F.U.B.A.R. circle jerk we've gotten our sorry asses into," I told him.

Dr. Construction and I had been serious running buddies since way back in the day. Just since first grade, really. That was long before we had tried to co-habitate with women and create children. All these years later, the children had worked out for both of us, just like their mothers had not. Now, recently reunited, the good Doctor and I had reached that zenith in life where we had money of our own and were beholden to no man. Sure, we could just sit by the pool smoking hashish and drinking margaritas, while young women too young for our hairstyles attended to our every need. Even that gets old, and a lot quicker than you might imagine. Doc sat studying the legal papers and the add-on attorney nonsense.

"You say it's this Harvey Mendelsohn that's all jammed up, right?"

"One and the same," I said. Doc made a clucking sound. This was a sure sign that his brain was springing into gear.

"Says here that the state's witness was one Ed Helms, formerly of Barstow, California, currently residing at 622 Esplanade,

Redondo Beach, California."

"Beach front, as I recall, Doc."

"Yeah, "didn't we both date the same gal lived in that building?"

"Golden memories are for old men," I reminded him.

"Yeah, so they say. It appears that ole Ed was the state's only witness and his testimony was the sole reason our man Harvey was convicted."

"Exactly why I told his sister that you and I would take the case."

"Barstow, hmm. Isn't that coming right up?"

Dr. Construction had always been a whiz at geography, even out of a dead sleep.

"You know how I feel about Barstow, Doc. My favorite uncle died there."

"Right, twenty years ago. It would be good to see where this guy, Helms started out. Interview a friend or two, get a fix on him. Besides, Frosty lives in Barstow now. We haven't seen him in years."

I flipped open the driver's hidden compartment and pulled out my trusty one hitter.

"Tell you what. We're about fifty miles from Barstow. I'm gonna have a medicinal hit and meditate on your suggestion. Frosty is always trouble, you know that."

"Trouble!" Doc protested.

"He was one of the gang before he went away."

I eased the Lincoln down to ninety-five. Traffic was picking up and the detector was singing to me about cops in the distance. Frosty had been a good friend and I had visited him in prison. Doc had not. (More on that later, since Doc's failure to visit is also related to his moniker.)

Frosty had been the victim of an overzealous prosecutor. Frosty's was just the kind of case Doc and I would've worked, had we been doing this back then. Frosty was guilty of driving his older brother Pacer to the liquor store to buy a six pack. Pacer was four years older than all of us and we learned at a very early age to steer clear of him. Already a speed freak, he had recently added reds to his diet. Very flaky. When he went ape shit in the liquor store and pumped the store owner full of slugs, his high had reached a new low. The old man behind the counter reminded him of his ex-father-in-law, or so Pacer said. Frosty sat outside, behind the wheel grooving to FM radio and enjoying a sunny day. The D.A. hit Frosty with "Accessory to Murder One." His brother, Pacer, got twenty to life, which wasn't enough in my opinion. Frosty got twenty and walked out after serving twelve years and ten months. Just long enough to lose his youth. He was twenty-nine when he went in and forty-three and graying when he left. I took one more hit of the O.G. Kush and thought about it. He HAD been one of us.

Frosty's house sat at the end of a cul-de-sac with a lot of space on either side. He had a large back yard which was ringed by dense woods. For five years breathing free air, he had done extremely well for himself.

"You think Frosty got himself a woman with money?" Doc asked.

"Hell," I said, "you talked to him last. We haven't exactly been close since he got out. Did he say he had an ole lady?"

"Oh, he's got an ole lady, sure. He just did not tell his good buddy she was one of the fortunate few." As the Lincoln completed the circle we realized that the home was even larger than it appeared at first glance. It was a new build. A mini-mansion in a square layout with a large open center.

"Did Frosty say what business he had gone into, Doc?"

"No, but I know what you're thinking."

"Yeah," I said. "Better do a quick surveil."

I kept the Lincoln below thirty-five as we covered the area. There were four streets that ended at the cul-de-sac. Any one of them could offer up a clear view of the house. Counter surveillance is a great start to a nutritious breakfast. Not only that, it's the main reason I had a new birthday this year. First block was clean. Second block was cle....

"Hold it, there he is. Blue house, on the right, check the driveway," I said.

"Sly bastard. Look, he's got a direct line on Frosty's front door."

"Sonovabitch," Doc said. "Dark blue, government-issue, Plymouth sedan. An under-cover hippie, if ever there was one. Light red hair and beard, can't make the plate, but I'll guaranfuckin' tee you he's got a set of high power binocs in his lap."

The agent had not made us and we continued. One block over, it was a less creative stake out. This time it was a brown Plymouth, parked on the street with two men in suits. One L.E.O. on your ass and you had trouble. Two was a lot more than just double the trouble and meant one of two things. 1) A non-cooperating Federal and local operation. Unlikely, but it happens. 2) Two or more government agencies as a joint task force preparing to serve a hostile warrant with a S.W.A.T. assault on a known felon, considered armed and dangerous.

We considered the possibilities as I pointed the Lincoln out of Frosty's neighborhood.

"A number two for sure," I said.

"Yeah, a real shitter."

Doc pulled up the GPS and we were in luck. The stand of trees in back of Frosty's house ran for about quarter of a mile and ended up behind someone else's mini-mansion. We found that house and parked up the street from it. Unlike Frosty, this man had no neighbors in his ready-made cul-de-sac kingdom. We armed ourselves. I slipped my holstered 9 mm into my waistband. Doc took his time getting control of his 357 Magnum. I knew he was making a show of it because of the comment I made when he packed it.

"Sure, I've got size issues," Doc said. "As a real man I'm not afraid to address it."

I stifled a laugh. One of the more lovable things about the ole buzzard -- he knew how to keep it loose in a serious situation. We separated in the woods and covered the quarter mile in a sweep. No sign of the Federals though. We stayed under cover and reconvened at the edge of Frosty's back yard and waited. Five minutes ticked by, then seven.

"Nobody back here," Doc whispered.

"Agreed. Electronic only, at this point, I'm guessing."

There was a stucco-type wall part way around the property that was under construction, but it appeared to have been abandoned. We each drew our weapon, looked at each other, and gave a low "Huzzah." Doc advanced twenty-five feet, and then I moved up. This way, we were never without cover. We were quickly at the over-sized, wooden back door. Doc chuckled and motioned toward the huge golden knocker positioned in the center of the door. Like everything else about the place it was bigger than life and a bit much for a rear door. Doc signaled me, pounded on it and we quickly flattened out on each side of the door. A beat, then an explosion, as a round of shotgun pellets sprayed a perfect circle through the door. Frosty knew the Federals were coming alright.

"Frosty, it's me, Indy and the Doctor's with me."

"Hey, Frankie, it's Doc."

"Nobody fuckin' calls me that anymore," Frosty screamed through the door. Doc and I both laughed. He hated his first name.

"Alright fuckheads, you so real. Who was our first grade

teacher?"

"Ms. Shonda Greene." Doc and I sang out. Whatever Frosty was screaming was smothered out by the sound of multiple bolts and locks being forced open.

The big door finally flew open and Doc and I rushed in. Frosty slammed it shut and motioned to a leggy blonde beauty that went to work securing all the locks. We stood in complete darkness except for the two flashlights they carried. This was odd since it was a bright day out. I soon realized that the windows in this part of the house had been automatically sealed to deny access when the trouble started. I'd never seen Frosty so happy. Frosty, who had never been a hugger, gave us each a long, tight squeeze. He patted me on the back so hard I thought I might have rib damage. Frosty didn't look much different, only taller than when I had last seen him, seven years earlier, inside Leavenworth's walls. Instead of his short and tight, marine-style haircut, he now sported a wild, bushy, red "fro."

"Well, saints are fuckin' the sinners tonight. Never thought I'd see you two this side of dirt," Frosty said.

"Yeah," Doc said. "What's up with all the visitors?"

"Sorry 'bout the buckshot," Frosty said, "but they cut the power not more than thirty seconds before you knocked." The blonde, who had finished her duties, joined us, sliding an arm around Frosty's waist. "Guys, this is my ole lady, Melinda." Frosty gave her a peck on the head.

"Our pleasure," I said. Doc and I did our double bow, which was wasted in the darkness.

Their flashlights started to move. Doc and I carefully followed the bouncing lights and stumbled along.

"Me and Melinda are on a schedule we gotta stick to. Generator was supposed to kick on when the power went and the window covers came down. Where should I start, Babe?" Frosty stopped, turned, shined his light up at his face and winked at Melinda. Melinda spoke as we resumed pace, "Fuck, Baby, ain't no place to start, 'cept the beginning. The whore sold us out."

"More common than you would believe," Doc jumped in. "Indy, tell 'em bout the one who got the drop on you that time in Mexi..."

"DOC," I yelled. "She wasn't a whore. Let Frosty talk, will ya?"

Frosty spoke up. "We live through the next forty five minutes, Doc, I wanna hear that story."

"A classic," Doc assured him.

"Hold up," Frosty said. We had stopped outside an open door. I could feel from the surface that the door was heavy-gauge steel. We followed them in. Frosty inched along, shining his light toward the wall in front of him. He popped open a utility box and fumbled around for a few seconds. Suddenly, bright, harsh light filled the room. Frosty turned a dial and hit a switch or two and the light remained, but softened.

"Half power's all we need," he said. Melinda, who was even more attractive now that I could see her more clearly, was already busy spinning a dial on another large metal door which, I figured, could only be a gun safe. I looked around. We stood in a panic room made of reinforced concrete and steel with battery-pack lights mounted near the ceiling. Melinda opened the two metal doors to reveal an entire gun room, not just a safe. Frosty racked the black-on-black shotgun he held.

"Let's load up with hardware; I got a treat for you two." He and Melinda stepped into the heavily armed room where guns, pistols, rifles, shotguns and even several R.P.G.'s lined the walls. Melinda picked out a shotgun like Frosty's and two .45's. Doc and I hadn't moved from the doorway of the fortress. Frosty looked over and we held our weapons up for inspection.

"Still packing heavy D, Doc. Good call," Frosty said. "Down at the end, there's ammo for both guns." We did as instructed, each grabbing a belt of ammo. "See that crate. Get us some masks out will ya?" Doc and I passed around the gas masks. Frosty said, "Go ahead and put 'em on, let 'em hang on your chest. We're gonna need 'em in a hurry." Frosty grabbed a walkie talkie with a microphone attached, lifted a heavy, fully loaded utility belt off a hook and strapped it around his waist. Since lots of tools and electronics hung there, it was apparent that he had stocked this Swiss Army belt at an earlier time. He led us back out the door, which was much easier going now that we had light.

As we made our way through several rooms it became clear that Melinda had a flair for decorating, even if it was early Grateful Dead in style. Finally, they led us into a large, great room with a fireplace as big as a VW beetle. Frosty had us assemble around an ornate teak card table.

"You were telling us," I reminded him.

"Would you believe law enforcement pussy tastes just as good as civilian pussy?" Frosty asked.

"I'm shocked," Doc replied.

"Amazing," I chimed in.

"Yeah," Frosty went on. "Me and Melinda, they say, sold to an undercover. Should a' known. Twenty -five year-old beauty queen wantin' to do an old con with bad teeth."

"Don't beat yourself up, hon, she snowed me too," Melinda said. I looked into her face. She couldn't have been more than thirty two herself.

"Look brother," Doc said. "Me and Indy got the top lawyers in the nation on speed dial. This sounds like entrapment. We could probably get you off." Doc knew as well as I did that entrapment as a legal defense didn't really exist anymore. It was the technique law enforcement used in most busts, often to great success.

"Yeah," I lied. "I like your chances. I'll call Ben Silverstein in New York. He's never lost a case." I whipped out my iPhone.

"No, don't call," Frosty spoke up. "Look, I appreciate it, I really do, but I'm fuckin' over this whole legal ballgame, besides, me and Melinda made a pact. So, let's celebrate." Frosty must have pushed a hidden button, because the teak surface split down the middle and slid out of sight. Under it was a glass covered compartment which quickly rose up to replace the teak. On it were four shiny, white, compressed rocks about an ounce each. At least twenty lines were splayed out in front of the rocks, ready to snort. I could tell from the sparkle that it was cocaine, not speed. I felt sad and depressed to find Frosty still stuck in the eighties.

"What kind of a pact?" Doc asked. "I don't like that, Frosty. It doesn't sound right." Frosty ignored Doc's question, handing him a gold-plated straw. Frosty bent forward and quickly made four long lines disappear. He stood up, twirled his silver straw in his hand, and smiled.

"We'll party 'til it don't matter. Whatta'ya say, Indy? You used to be a coke connoisseur." Frosty handed me the silver straw while Melinda was doing her part to hoover the table.

"Thanks buddy, I'm trying to quit," I told him, feeling a bit hypocritical with the speed I had taken earlier buzzing 'round my brain. Doc had already laid the golden straw down on the table. He hadn't snorted anything stronger than Jack Daniels in at least fifteen years. He put his hand on Frosty's shoulder.

"Back this truck up a minute, brother. We joke around a lot but we're for real. This day and age, couple a grams of coke, no problem." Melinda raised her head up from the table and let out a laugh that would've made a hyena nervous. Frosty chuckled.

"Ten metric tons actually, buddy." Doc, for once, was silenced.

I kept thinking back to the early days when everyone thought cocaine was the real deal, harmless fun, a great social high. I remember a doctor friend had brought an eight ball of cocaine to my birthday party. Of course, everybody who stayed with coke eventually crashed and burned. Bankruptcy, divorce, addiction, even prison for a couple of people we knew. What the hell. Frosty wasn't in the joint then. He saw all that happen. Then I flashed on something Frosty had said when I last visited him behind the wall. "Prison can make you forget a lot of things." Of course I was thinking about the touch of a woman when he said that. That kind of thing. Suddenly, I understood what he meant. While I zoned out to memory lane, our hosts had poured us all a drink from the well-stocked bar nearby. Frosty laughed like we were at a garden party with nothing but beer on our minds.

"So Carlos Lehder was my celly. Saved his life before his guys got there."

"THE Carlos Lehder?" Doc asked, "The transportation king of the Medellin cartel?"

"Yeah, I've got him to thank for all this," Frosty said. The sound of breaking glass startled us. A hissing sound followed.

"Front dining room window," Melinda yelled out. Frosty hit a button behind the bar. Steel doors sealed both doorways into the large room. The wall in front of us slid up into the ceiling and was quickly replaced with TV monitors, each with a different angle of the exterior. Every monitor was black with helmets and bullet-proof vests. L.E.O.'s of every size shape and agency, Federal and local, were coiled and ready to strike. Frosty scanned the monitors then tugged at the gas mask hanging on his chest. "Keep em handy."

"Those fucks," Melinda yelled.

"Gonna be real surprised they come waltzin' in here," Frosty said. "By the way, Doc, I might need you to inspect some of my demo work." I could see Doc wince.

"You do have another way out a here right?" Doc asked. A loud amplified voice broke in.

"This is Lt. Dan Walters, Federal Resolution Team. I'm here to help. Just follow my instructions so nobody gets hurt." Frosty grabbed the mic attached to the radio on his belt. His voice boomed out even louder than Walters', our new friendly Fed buddy.

"Nice of you tossing the gas on us, Walt. Could you send in some food? I'd like steak. Honey, whatta you wan..."

"In good faith," Walters cut in, "I'm going to allow your two new guests safe passage. They have five minutes to surrender themselves out the front door. Otherwise they'll be considered armed combatants and treated as such." Frosty was ready.

"Gotta call my mom and see what she thinks. Gimme fifteen minutes." A long pause followed, and then Lt. Walters was back.

"I should inform you, sir. We cut all communications into the house, including cellular. I am arranging a throw phone for you right now. I'll get back to you." Frosty hung up his mic.

"That ain't even neighborly. Should I tell him I got my own system, Babe?" Melinda was vigorously chewing on a plastic straw while working another one between her fingers, knuckle to knuckle. She had been marching around the room deep in thought. I could tell this was Frosty's attempt to reel her back in. Melinda seemed to snap out of her trance. I wasn't sure if it was coke-induced or a product of the situation we found ourselves in. Maybe both. Melinda crossed the room, rushed up to Frosty and grabbed the satellite phone off his belt.

"I gotta call my mom. Fuck him." Melinda turned, punching in numbers as she walked back across the room. Frosty stood watching her go. Static and the voice of our favorite Fed killed our quiet.

"I've got a phone on the way. My man is dropping it through the dining room window. Don't fire on him." We watched two of

Walters' men on the monitor lining up a potato shooter at the dining room window. Frosty keyed his mic again.

"You send in that cunt, aka Darlene Little, for just five minutes, this whole thing'll be over. I promise you that."

"That's not going to happen, you know that," Walters barked back. The sound of more breaking glass interrupted him and then Walters spoke again.

"That was just the phone. Everybody stay calm."

Frosty yelled to Melinda, "Tell her you'll call her right back." It took a bit and Frosty had to get in her face but Melinda finally hung up the Sat phone. "When we go through in a minute, pick up their phone and call her back," Frosty told her. Then Frosty got back on his P.A. system. "Thanks, my ole lady's got to call her mom, and then it'll be my turn. We need fifteen minutes."

"I like that," Walters said. "I'll give you ten. What about your buddies?" Frosty smiled at us.

"They decided to stay," he barked back.

"Okay, time starts now," Walters informed us.

"Got it," Frosty bellowed back. Out of habit, I set my iPhone timer alarm and, from the corner of my eye, I could see Frosty click a button on his watch. As I looked around the room I marveled at the steel doors keeping the gas out and the high tech monitors. He must have cameras covering every inch of the exterior. Frosty had truly thought of everything when designing this house, or had he?

Frosty walked to the door, "Get your masks on. We're goin' down stairs; we gotta cut through the gassed area." I pulled my mask up and checked that my seal was secure. Doc did the same. Frosty hit a button by the steel door and the door slid out of sight. Frosty spoke through his mask.

"There's a supply tunnel goes back up into those woods you guys came in from. I need Doc to check my charges are set right, and then you guys are out."

Even through the mask I could see the disgusted look on Doc's face. His original nickname had been Dr. Destruction. Unlike me, Doc joined the army straight out of high school. With his proclivity for blowing things up, he was soon in the Army's Ordnance Corps in Ft. Lee, Virginia. In fact, Doc was so successful at blasting shit to shinola that he went from the Army to doing special Ops work in parts unknown for the CIA. Later, he went from Agency employee to ultra-successful contractor when he started his own demolition company. He got his share of legitimate government contracts, but his real rep was built on urban hi-rise and casino bring downs. In fact, if you saw a controlled, Vegas casino demolition on TV in the nineties that was Doc's work. His company dropped the old hotels in their own footprint while leaving nearby skyscrapers untouched. In 1998, Doc's nephew, his sister's only son, was killed when a worker set a charge wrong. The young man had only been working one month after graduating from college. Within twenty-four hours, Doc sold his demolition company.

He already had a small construction firm that built commercial buildings, so he focused exclusively on that. By the time he turned it over to his son it was billing several million dollars a year. The Dr. Destruction name had that super villain sound and I do miss calling him that. But, out of respect for his nephew, we don't use it anymore. Dr. Construction fits him better now anyway.

Doc never visited Frosty or anybody else in the joint for a very good reason. The one time he did go behind prison walls he couldn't quit focusing on the weakest points in the structure. He would quickly diagram in his mind the best spots to place the C-4 and charges for the jail break. Frosty hit another button at the end of the hallway and that steel door slid back into the wall. I was surprised that the gas rushing in was still so thick. Visibility was very low, even though this part of the house had natural light streaming in from non-shuttered windows. We followed Frosty and Melinda through three rooms, stopping in the dining room long enough to help Melinda find the drop phone.

"Remember," Frosty said. "Tell her nothin' you don't want the Feds to know." Melinda quickly dialed her mom again as we walked. We were out of the gas now and Frosty led us down a long stairway to the basement. I pulled my mask off and looked around. Unlike the floors above that were filled wall to wall with furniture and decorations, the basement was almost empty. There was a storage shed, the outdoor type, and several wooden pallets. Doc nodded toward the far wall where the oddest thing sat. It looked like a shiny, modern-day version of a 1950's coal bucket. The kind miners used way back in the fifties to haul coal, supplies and miners in and out of the mines. It was made of clean, silver steel. Instead of wheels, it had an odd assortment of hooks, levers and pulleys on its bottom.

"That your supply cart, Frosty?" Doc asked. Frosty smiled big.

"That bucket has kept the entire Southwest high and happy for the last few years. Gonna be your Greyhound out a here."

I watched Melinda walk in circles, the drop phone pressed to her ear. At the rate she was talking, her mom could only listen. Frosty led us over to the front left corner of the room.

"See it Doc?" Doc stepped closer and peered down at a gray backpack. He kept his eye on it while he moved to the left and then the right. Doc finally eased toward it and dropped to his knees. I looked at my alarm. We had used up four of Walters' minutes. Six minutes left. I looked at the far right corner and spotted another backpack. Doc lifted the flap of the one in front of him. I could see a short fuse and some wires. Doc felt around a bit, adjusted its position, then closed the flap and stood back up.

"Well?" Frosty asked. Doc crossed his arms and took a long look around the basement room. All four corners had a blast pack.

"Wired to one detonator?" he asked.

"In my pocket," Frosty said.

"Oh, it'll do the job and then some," Doc assured him. "Two of them would've been overkill." Doc paused as he surveyed the room again. "Gonna move a ton of dirt. Leave em' all set for a new lake, just add water." Frosty threw his head back and laughed a deep cleansing laugh. I was not laughing and I spoke up.

"All these guys out front will be killed," I said. "Think about it, brother, these are just men like you and me with kids and car payments and bitchy ole ladies at home."

"They're on the wrong damn team," Frosty barked. Doc rocked from one foot to the other on the balls of his feet.

"This ain't you, Frost. You're the guy that never wanted to hit guys too hard in football," Doc said. Melinda ran up to Frosty and stretched up toward him on her tip toes. He bent down and kissed her. "Babe, let them take the painting out, please," she said. Frosty laughed again.

"We were fucking kids, Doc. That was before I got fucked by the world. Sure, go get it," he told her. Melinda led us to the little storage shed.

"Yeah, Carlos gave me this a couple a years ago," Frosty continued. "Sort of a job well done kind a thing, I guess. It's a painting of two hookers lined up to get their VD shot."

"Lehder got life plus, how's he sending you paintings?" Doc asked.

"Somebody else is doin' his time. He's still the king of transport; he just moves it for the agency now. He's out of San Francisco mostly," Frosty said. For the second time today, both Doc and I were stumped. Melinda slid a wooden-crated painting out of the shed. We couldn't see the painting itself. She looked up at me.

"Please take care of it. It's real art, a classic."

"Yeah," Frosty chuckled. "Painted by that French midget. Carlos got it in payment for a whole plane load." I looked at my phone alarm.

"Three minutes left, guys." I grabbed a side of the painting. It wasn't very heavy. Melinda and I carried it over next to the bucket and rested it against the wall. Frosty hit a button and what had just been a concrete wall moved to reveal a tunnel. A modern day, steel tunnel with lights and smooth walls. It had a railroad track like set of rails in the floor running as far as the eye could see. Doc helped Frosty lift the bucket up onto the steel rails in the floor. One pull backward and it was locked onto the system. We loaded the painting in. We heard movement upstairs.

"Son of a bitch," Frosty said. He pulled his shotgun up and fired at the top of the stairwell, blasting the door apart. He racked the gun and fired again. The movement upstairs stopped. I looked at my phone.

"Yeah, I show two minutes left," I said.

"Fuckin' liars," Melinda screamed. Doc gave me a slight nod and a look as I edged toward Frosty while Doc stepped slowly behind him. Out of nowhere, Frosty rammed his shotgun backward plunging the stock into Doc's stomach. The sudden blow sent Doc down. Frosty raised the gun, pointing it at my eye level. Doc rolled around, fighting to catch his breath on the floor.

"You two been usin' that juke move since eighth-grade basketball, Indy. You think I'd go down on that ole fake?" He backed up, still leveling the shotgun.

"Help him up. You two gotta roll."

"We had to try, brother," I told him. I helped Doc up, pulled most of his weight onto my back and dragged him to the bucket. Doc raised his head and looked back at Frosty.

Between his gasps for air, Doc said, "You deserve a helluva lot better from this world, Frosty. Come with us." Melinda stood next to Frosty now. I saw the detonator in his hand, his thumb poised over the plunger. I helped Doc into the bucket, then I jumped into the other side. The crated painting sat wedged between us. Bullets ripped through the ceiling from upstairs, peppering the stairwell. Melinda returned fire with her shotgun and pistol. I looked back at Frosty. His attention was turned toward the stairwell. I quickly jumped to the lip of the bucket and dove. Arching and stretching as far as I possibly could, I landed right on top of Frosty, driving him to the floor. His head seemed to do a slow-mo bounce against the concrete and the detonator clattered across the floor. I rolled off him and jumped up, ready for a fight but he was out cold from the blow his head took from the concrete.

"What the fuck?" Melinda asked. I checked Frosty's vitals and he was fine, just out. Melinda was crying.

"He'll be okay," I told her. Doc, who had followed me out of the bucket, put his arm around her shoulder.

"You don't wanna die here, right?" Doc asked.

"No, that was Frosty's idea," she said, her lip trembling. In no time, we had loaded Frosty's unconscious body into the bucket. We rested his head in Melinda's lap. I started for the detonator but Doc told me we didn't need it.

"The way he set those charges, one stray bullet and this place is blown to hell." Right on time, a bullet blasted into the outside of the cart as others began bouncing and ricocheting all around us. SWAT guys were now at the top of the stairs. I laid down a ring of fire with my 9, blasting out the fifth step and forcing SWAT to find reverse, while Doc grabbed Frosty's mic.

"Walters, pull your men. This place is wired to explode." Walters' reply was quick and loud.

"We don't respond to threats."

Doc looked at me. "Touchy ain't he?" He went back on the mic. "Walters, this... this is not Frosty, alright? I'm trying to save lives here. Pull your men out."

Again Walters took it as a boast. Doc yelled out one more plea, loud and clear as I hit the green button for the track. The bucket jerked forward forcefully, knocking me on to my face and Doc backward to the metal floor. The bucket lurched again then sped forward at lightning speed. We were pinned to the wall of the bucket on a roller coaster ride from hell. I stuck my head up to see where we might be headed but the rushing wind warped my eye lids closed. I heard, and felt a loud explosion and looked behind us. A ball of fire erupted, chasing us up the track. Another louder explosion rumbled up the track behind us. The heat from the approaching fire was singeing my eyebrows and about to engulf us. The little bucket hit warp speed and suddenly we left it all behind. Just then the bucket slowed, angled upward a few feet, and came to a peaceful stop like it had never been doing a hundred and ten. Six Flags had nothing on this roller coaster.

I shook my head trying to get my mind to catch up to my body. We seemed to have rolled into the dining room of a very finely furnished home.

"Get out quick," Doc yelled as he dived out of the bucket and helped Melinda out behind him. I pushed the crated painting over the side and grabbed hold of Frosty's shoulders. He moaned but was still dreaming. Just then, a rumble below us knocked me over. I struggled up again to see Doc pulling Frosty over the side of the cart. I pushed his body upward and finally lifted him by his boots. We dropped him over and I jumped out afterward. Melinda was able to slide the painting across the carpet. We had dragged Frosty only about three feet when another rumble and then a series of shock waves shook the whole house. Doc and I were thrown off our feet and ended up in a pile with Frosty. A huge explosion erupted underneath us. I looked over at the bucket. A molten stream of fire enveloped the bucket and blasted it upward, sending it hurtling through the roof. The entire frame of the house was lifted up off its foundation and then crashed back down. Windows shattered outward and the house creaked and groaned for a bit. Then things for the first time got quiet and became still. Doc and I joined Melinda who was staring out the blown-out window at the back of the dining room. She stood frozen in shock. An orange ball of fire lit up the other side of the woods where the house had been. I mumbled an old Sioux warrior's prayer for those men we had left behind. It seemed the rubble of Frosty's old house was still ablaze along with some of the trees that had been at the end of their back yard. We heard sporadic gunfire as rounds from Frosty's arsenal continued to overheat and explode. There was another soul-shuddering rumble. The foundation of the house we were in shook again. Through the woods we could see another giant fireball erupt as a thunderous roar flattened our ear drums and extinguished the orange blaze. Only a small fire remained.

As a thousand sirens started, I realized I could barely hear them. I opened my mouth, stretched my jaw from side to side and then held my nose while pushing air into my ears. It didn't help. Everything still sounded like it was coming out of a speaker dialed down to one. We looked around and surveyed the damage to our new abode. For the first time, I realized we were inside the lone Mc-mansion in the cul-de-sac where we had parked the Lincoln. Doc turned to Melinda. "So this was Frosty's stash house?"

"We built both places at the same time," Frosty answered, his voice drifting in from behind us. Melinda turned, squealing like a teenager and jumped into Frosty's arms. I gave Doc a 'get ready' look. Frosty hugged Melinda long and hard like he couldn't let her go. When he raised his head, I could see tears in his eyes.

"Thanks, guys. I must have gone crazy." Doc smiled, no doubt relieved we weren't going to have to go two more rounds with the champ. We both got hugs from the big guy.

"You can always rebuild what you had," I said. We started to walk through the other rooms. The decor looked familiar. Melinda laughed.

"That Lautrec you helped us carry out is worth fourteen mil, give or take. I looked it up on Google." Doc and I stared at the crate.

"Damn Frosty, you meant a Toulouse-Lautrec whorehouse?" I asked.

"Told ya that," Frosty said. Doc and I looked at each other.

"Oh, that French midget," we replied in unison.

"What you're sayin' though, Indy, it makes sense," Frosty said.

"What?" Doc asked, "About the French midget?"

"No, the rebuilding, the starting over. I'm officially dead, right?" Frosty asked.

"It might take a few days on the official part," Doc said.

"So give it a week. It don't matter. I got a new chance." I could see Frosty's eyes light up as a new scheme was being born. I looked out through the shattered front window to see the trusty old Lincoln parked right where we had left it. Otherwise, the street was empty. It was clear that Frosty and company owned the other empty lots in the cul-de-sac.

"We'll back the Lincoln up into the garage, just to be safe. Can't have anyone seeing you," I said to Frosty.

"Me and Melinda will haul the picture down," Frosty said. Doc and I looked out the window. We went out the front door and down the steps.

"Really wasn't a midget you know," I told Doc.

"Course he was," Doc said. "He painted because he got sexually frustrated when he couldn't have the sultry show girls he got drunk with." I pointed the remote at the Lincoln and was satisfied to hear the B-e-e-n-k sound in response.

"You're saying he was a great artist because he had a perpetual hard-on?" I asked.

"There ya go," Doc said. "Twisting my words again." We were almost to the car. "Good thing I found this parking spot for ya, huh?" Doc said.

I said, "Yeah, Doc, I really wanted to kill twenty Federal agents and run up a few felonies before breakfast. I just needed a place to park." Doc gave me his impatient look. (*We were later relieved to find out that not a single agent had died in the explosion. Walters had pulled all but two men at our first warning. Those last two had cleared the house in time and escaped with minor injuries.*)

"You're taking this too seriously, Indy. We didn't kill anybody. We warned them. Technically you could say Frosty is guilty, but hell, he's going to show up dead in their records. They can't prosecute a stiff." I could feel my bullshit-meter red line.

"Ever fuckin' occur to you, Doctor, that maybe ole Frost has gotten just a little too high on his own supply? He says his coke supplier is Carlos Lehder. The cocaine king that's been in Federal lockup since oh, I don't know… the late eighties?" I opened the door of the Lincoln and slid into the familiar leather driver's seat while Doc grabbed his spot.

"Not the first time," Doc said as he closed his door. "Agency needs somebody that's up on life, they replace that guy with a Filler and their man walks. Just depends on how much National Security is at stake." I turned and looked at Doc for a minute.

"A Filler?" I asked. "So common they have a name for it?"

"Well, you know," Doc said. I shook my head in disbelief.

"Frosty and Melinda will need new IDs. Plus, how long 'til the Feds find out we were the house guests?" I asked.

"They don't need to know that," Doc said. "I can turn a screw or two to make sure they don't. Hell, I'll just use the same old contact to get Frosty and Melinda new papers."

"Turn a screw or two? C'mon, Doc, you need to put a little more uncertainty into your voice," I said.   "What the hell's that supposed to mean?" Doc asked.

"It means Barstow was something you already had worked out. With a lot of agency help," I said, as I put the key in the ignition. "You knew, didn't you?" I asked.

"Knew what?" Doc asked.

"You knew Frosty was goin' down and I'm betting it was the agency that wanted Frosty out," I told him. Doc curled up one side of his lip, Elvis style.

"Indy, life's short. We agreed to grab all the rock and roll. Remember?"

I turned the key and the sound of the Lincoln springing to life gave me hope.

"Damn it, Doc. We're partners; I just like to know when I'm not working for myself. That's all. I am right though, right?" A sly grin crept across Doc's face.

"Actually, it was the painting they needed. Encoded message on the back or something. I just figured you and me owed Frosty one." Doc said. I laughed.

"Not anymore we don't." I turned my head over my shoulder so I could back into the driveway. Doc chuckled.

"Just be careful backing up, Indy, this Lincoln's the only pure thing we have left in the world."

ABOUT THE AUTHOR

Born with a taste for adventure Gary left Kansas City at 17 for that mythical land called Hollywood. While in college he worked as a cabbie on the west LA night shift and also tended bar at the Bel-Air Country Club. These two jobs provided in person adventures and stories full of enough Hollywood stars And true characters to last a lifetime. By age 22 Gary had been fortunate enough to work behind the scenes in production on two very iconic feature films.

After College he worked as a professional photographer specializing in fashion and travel which took him all over the world. Gary soon expanded into video production producing music videos and TV commercials.

Gary experienced some of his best adventures as an apprentice with an Indian Medicine Man. Also when he was videographer for a small dedicated team of mercenaries fighting for human rights in Central America.

Along the way Gary developed and programmed channels for cable television where he also hosted entertainment shows. He has owned sales companies in real estate, insurance and advertising.

In 2008 after years of studying the craft of screen-writing, he optioned his first screenplay. Since that time he has dedicated himself to writing full time. He currently has two film projects in development. Gary splits his time between southern Missouri and southern California where his mantra is "keep writing baby".

Thank You for reading. I hope you have enjoyed my stories.

All comments and questions are welcomed. You can email me at:

gary@loveyababy.info

To be notified about promotions, parties & the release date of the upcoming novel in 2013 please join our newsletter on the Love Ya Baby site.

Website: loveyababy.info

Twitter: @garysanders1 and @loveyababy_gs1

thegarysandershow.com